WOLVES OF THE BEYOND

FROST WOLF

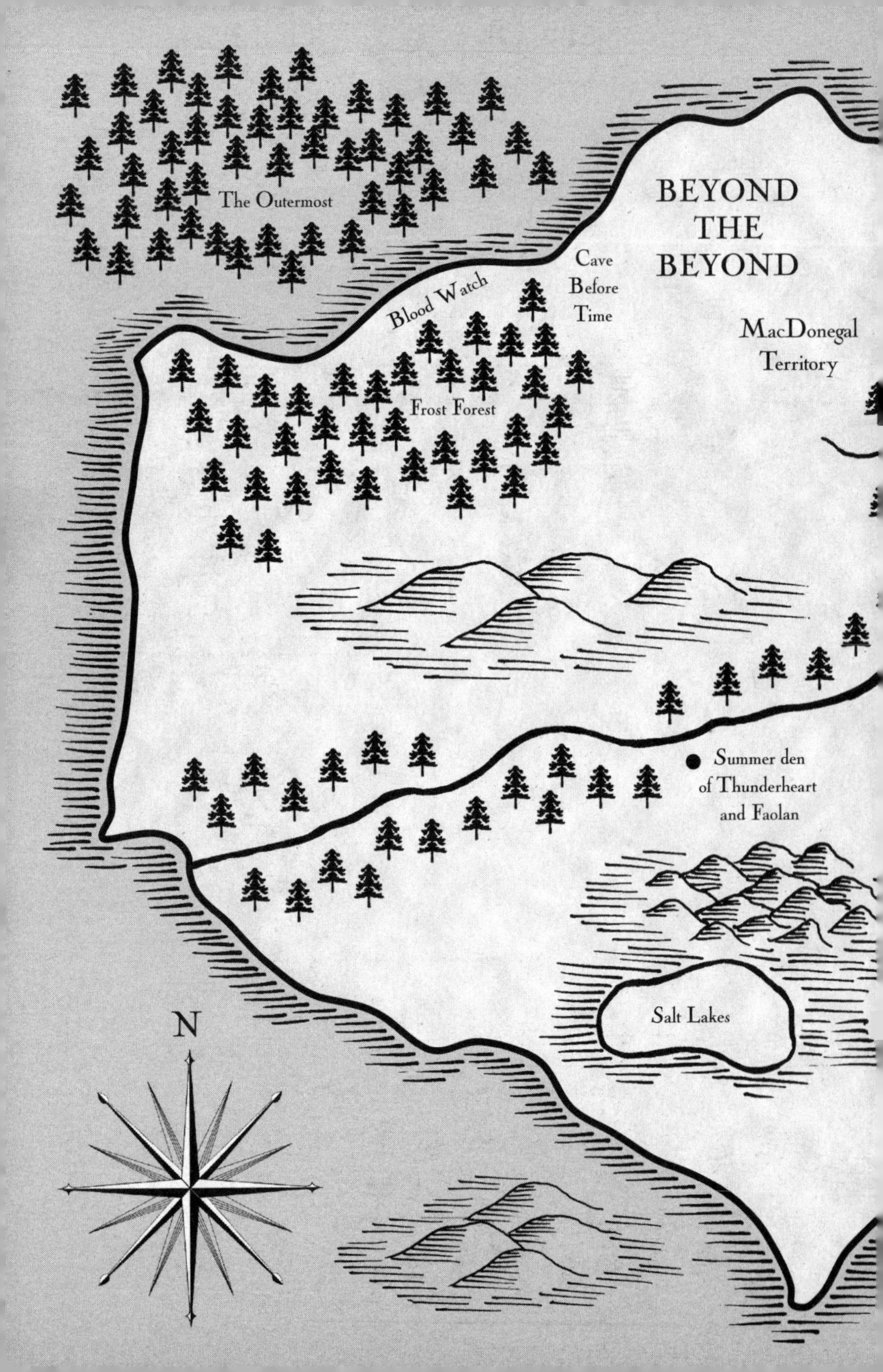

The Outermost

BEYOND THE BEYOND

Cave Before Time

Blood Watch

MacDonegal Territory

Frost Forest

Summer den of Thunderheart and Faolan

Salt Lakes

N

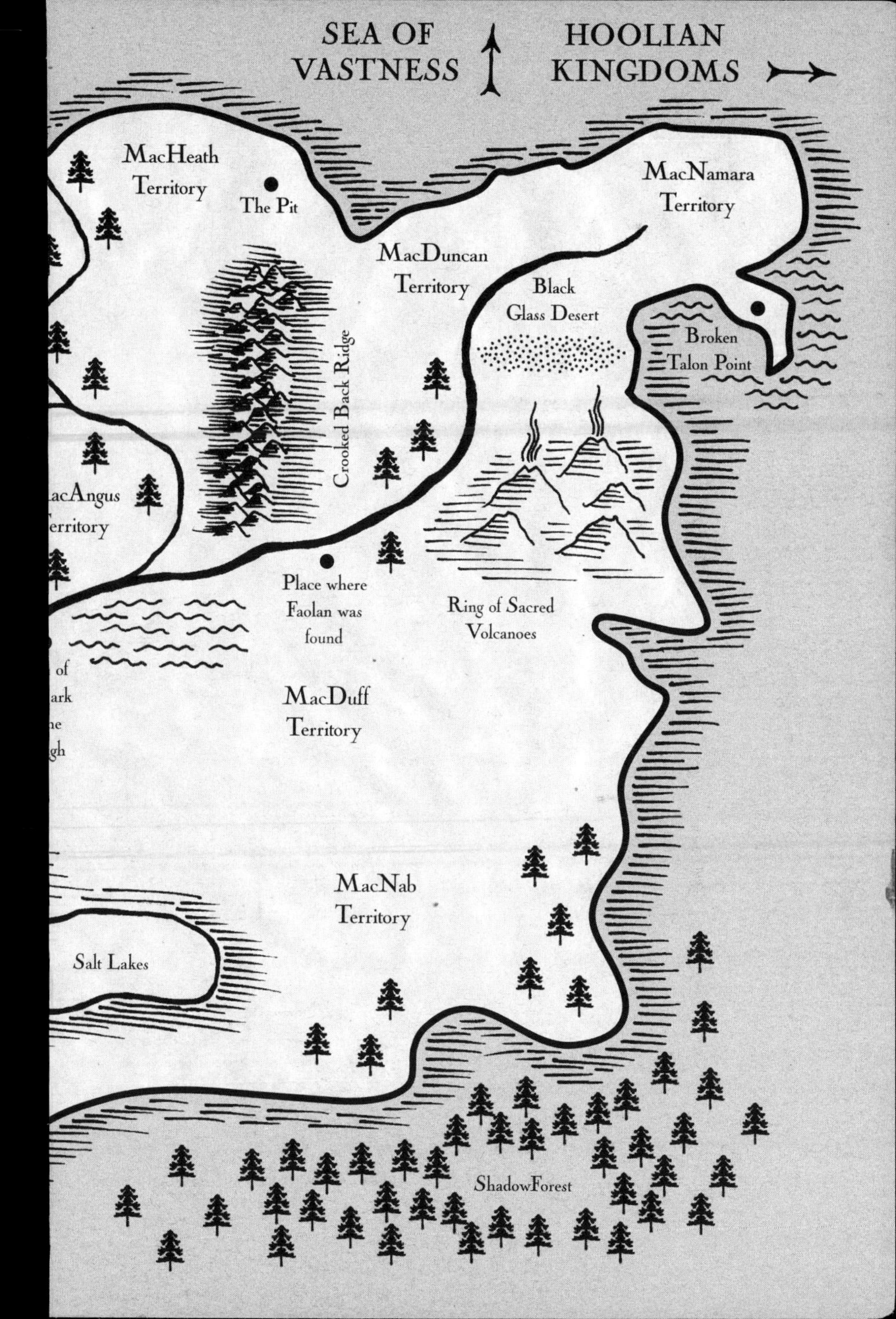
SEA OF VASTNESS
HOOLIAN KINGDOMS
MacHeath Territory
The Pit
MacNamara Territory
MacDuncan Territory
Black Glass Desert
Broken Talon Point
Crooked Back Ridge
Place where Faolan was found
Ring of Sacred Volcanoes
MacDuff Territory
MacNab Territory
Salt Lakes
ShadowForest

KATHRYN LASKY

WOLVES OF THE BEYOND
FROST WOLF

SCHOLASTIC PRESS / NEW YORK

For Rachel Griffiths

ISBN 978-0-545-43678-6

10 9 8 7 6 5 4 3 2 1 12 13 14 15 16

Printed in the U.S.A. 40
This edition first printing, January 2012

Map illustration by Lillie Howard
Book design by Lillie Howard

CONTENTS

The Old Buck

HE COULD HEAR THE POUNDING of their hearts behind him. The caribou herd, young and old alike, was struggling through the blinding gale of snow and sleet. The memory of the trail was inscribed deep within the old buck's muscles from years of leading. He knew the way as his father had known the way, and his grandfather, and back into the dim reaches of time. They had done this migration forever, but now he was confused, deeply confused. The old caribou had been leading the herd in circles for days, ever since the blizzard began.

All of the usual signposts had vanished under the onslaught of the gale. But they had started north at the right time, at the time of the Moon of New Antlers. Then something had gone wrong. As the herd traveled north, the seasons had traveled backward, or had winter never left? But why would the herd's antlers have dropped if it was not the time of the spring moons? Nothing made any sense.

The old buck felt as though he and his herd were teetering on the edge of doom. He would not go down in the ordinary way, toppled by a younger, stronger buck. This was not to be the death of him, but the death of all of them. The death of the herd. He could hear them now braying in baffled disbelief. *Where are we going? Where are the lichens, where is the summer grass? Where are you leading us?*

And the old buck dared not say that he was no longer leading them. For the vast, barren reaches of the Beyond eluded him, and round and round through the woods he continued to wander in circles without a trace of sweet summer grasses. The succulent mosses and lichens of the summer feeding grounds became dim memories.

CHAPTER ONE

FROST WOLF

SHE HEARD THE TREES OUTSIDE THE cave lean into the wind, groaning with despair. Edme, a Watch wolf of the Beyond, had never been in such thickly forested country before. Nor had she been so far from the glowing nimbus of the Ring of Sacred Volcanoes since her service on the Watch began. But these were peculiar times, and now she wondered if the despair she heard in the creaking trees was simply an invention of her mind.

She mused on this notion while she waited for Faolan to return from scouting. She was supposed to have been sleeping until her turn came to go out and look for tracks. Tracks of the herds that had never returned to the Beyond, herds of caribou or lone travelers like moose or elk. But the animals had disappeared. The meat trail of the past summers had almost vanished. Ordinarily, by this moon there would have been a dozen or more herds passing through the extended territory of the Ring of Sacred Volcanoes, and ten times that through the rest of the Beyond. But there had been only one herd so far, and the occasional stray. Wolf clans had to travel farther and farther to hunt, for the meat trail was dwindling. Might it simply vanish entirely?

It was summer! Summer, the time of meat. That was what made it all the more puzzling. The Moon of the Flies was upon them and yet the flies, too, had disappeared. The weather seemed to stutter between the hunger moons of winter and the raw, wet days of the Cracking Ice Moon, the first moon of spring. One day brought warmth and then the next brought freezing rain or even snow. The ice on the rivers hadn't really begun to crack until the Moon of New Antlers, months later than it should have. And even then the ice seemed to hang on desperately. The Moon of New Antlers was supposed to bring the warm winds. But instead it brought ice storms, the last of which had backed into the Moon of the Flies. Behind it was a weather front that threatened a real blizzard, with clouds thickening and casting a glowering light over the Beyond. The sun was becoming as elusive as the meat trail.

Occasionally the wolves had come across a lone caribou. But a single caribou, not even as large as a moose or an elk, could hardly provide enough meat to feed a pack, let alone a clan. And why would a caribou travel alone? They were herd animals.

With the dwindling supply of meat came rumors as well of small violations of clan territorial boundaries. Perhaps most shocking of all, there were stories of clans not sharing information with one another, through scent posts or howling, about sightings of animals or herds on mutual borders. This was bad. And it had resulted, Edme realized, in the oddest change of all: a terrible silence in the Beyond.

Everything in the Beyond depended upon communication among the wolf packs that made up the clans, and among the clans themselves. It was the *skreeleens* who howled out the messages from pack to pack and clan to clan, telling of a passing herd of caribou, or a moose brought down by a bear who would share the kill. Now there was a great engulfing silence that stretched across the Beyond, as if every wolf were listening, hoping that a *skreeleen* would announce the arrival of a herd, the sighting of an elk, a moose, anything. If such meat had been spotted, had the *skreeleens* been ordered not to howl? Was this silence caused by a terrible fear that famine might be coming?

Edme was suddenly aware of a presence just outside the cave. Then the darkness melted and a glowing form appeared before her. She inhaled sharply. It was a wolf, but like none she had ever seen. Huge and radiant but old, so old. A *lochin*! She felt her marrow freeze. Then a strangled bark cut the frigid air.

CHAPTER TWO

TRACKS TO NOWHERE

"URSKADAMUS TINE SMYORFIN MASACH!" Edme wasn't sure what to believe now — her ears or her eye? There was only one wolf who swore in both the language of bears and that of Old Wolf.

"Faolan?"

"Who else, for the love of Lupus? One would think you saw a ghost."

"But with all that frost — you look like a *lochin*."

Faolan gave a dismissive bark.

"You should see yourself," Edme persisted. "You've got icicles hanging from your chin fur. Your belly fur looks as if it's . . ."

"I know! I know! I can feel it!" he replied crankily.

"You look absolutely ancient. I mean older than the Sark."

"Thanks a lot," Faolan huffed.

"Well, what did you find?"

"No meat." His voice dwindled.

"I'll set out now. Maybe I'll have some luck."

Faolan seemed to hesitate, then said abruptly, "I'll go with you."

"It's not your turn. What's the sense in that?"

"I have to show you something that" — he hesitated again — "that makes no sense."

Edme came closer and cocked her head. "Faolan, what are you talking about?"

"It's disturbing. I can't quite describe it. But you have to see it."

"But you need to rest, Faolan. Neither one of us has eaten since yesterday, and that snow hare we caught was barely enough to feed a pup."

"It doesn't matter," he snapped. "Edme, I have to go with you. We have to look at this together." He looked straight into her single green eye.

"All right. All right, but first rest a bit."

The moon was a smear behind the scrim of heavily falling snow as they traveled to the edges of the Shadow

Forest on the far southeastern border between the Beyond and the Hoolian kingdoms. It was not a blizzard yet, but it seemed to be building to one. A blizzard in the Moon of the Flies!

They kept a deliberate pace at snow-paw speed, with their toes spread far apart so as not to sink into the powder. Their spindly legs seemed to float over the building drifts. The snow thickened and fell with an unswerving determination. Although Edme was just a few paces behind Faolan, there were moments when he was all but swallowed by the swirling snow. She lost sight of him entirely for several seconds. Faolan also frequently turned to look back over his shoulder and could feel his marrow clutch when he couldn't see Edme behind him. It was as if they had fallen into a void. As if the Beyond had broken open and they were tumbling into an abyss of infinite cold.

When they caught sight of each other they were relieved, but it felt to Edme as if she were reliving that first glimpse of Faolan when he had returned to the den. He had seemed so much like a ghost, but there was something else that frightened her even more. Despite his exceedingly large size — Faolan was a third again as big as most wolves — he had looked frail. Even ancient.

What occupied Faolan's thoughts were the strange tracks he had found. The creek they crossed was frozen, but Faolan thought that the ice seemed thinner in places. *Might there be a place we can break through for fish?* he wondered. The fish would be slow now, hardly swimming under the cold lock of the surface ice.

Later, Faolan admonished himself and pushed notions of food away. It helped him when he thought of bears and how they never felt the slightest twinge of hunger during their long, cold sleep of winter. Their hearts slowed and their minds became thick with dreams. But now it was summer, and what would the bears do? They couldn't sleep all year without starving.

"Here!" Faolan said abruptly. "Stop!"

"What?"

"I don't want you to disturb the tracks."

"What tracks?" Edme asked.

The impressions were faint but still visible.

"They are caribou tracks. Lots of them!" he replied.

Edme spotted them and began pressing her nose close to the snow to follow the tracks. She wagged her head slightly from side to side as she traced the dim scent. Faolan watched her. Within a short time she was back to where the tracks had started.

"I don't understand," she said. "It seems as if they are going in circles through this wood."

"They are. Or were," Faolan answered.

"A buck — from the tracks. My guess is an old buck was leading them. It looks as if he was staggering." She paused. "But in circles?"

"I know."

"Where did they go?" Edme asked.

"That I don't know. The tracks just vanish."

Like the trees that seemed to groan wretchedly in the night, the caribous' hoofprints seemed also to mark a deep anguish. The snow suddenly ceased and the moon appeared with a scalding brightness. The caribou tracks became more visible and more tantalizing. Faolan and Edme stared down at them, with the same thought as their mouths watered — *If only they led to something, a herd, a feeble cow.* It seemed like a cruel joke. An old, staggering buck leading his herd to nowhere. Their stomachs rumbled.

CHAPTER THREE

The Last Moose

AFTER INVESTIGATING THE TRACKS, Faolan returned to the den to rest, but Edme continued on her scouting expedition in hopes of picking up more of the caribou herd's trail. Her efforts proved futile, and as dawn broke the next morning, the two wolves set out toward the Ring of Sacred Volcanoes.

"Let's cross the creek here. I think the ice might be thinner and we could get some fish," Faolan suggested.

It did not take them long to claw through the ice, and within minutes they found three winter-thin salmon.

"It seems wrong catching them when they can barely move. It's not a fair fight exactly, and they hardly have any flesh on them." Edme shook her head as she swallowed the last piece.

"Eat the head. Thunderheart always made me eat it. She said it was the most nourishing part."

Edme shuddered. The notion of a fish head after the promise of meat from the caribou tracks was revolting.

"Go on! Eat it," Faolan growled.

"You even sound like a grizzly," Edme muttered as she took a small nip of the fish head.

"I could do worse," Faolan chuckled.

Thunderheart, a grizzly bear, had been Faolan's second Milk Giver. He had been cast out by the wolf clan, deemed a cursed one, and left to die because of his splayed paw. The grizzly had rescued him from an ice floe in the river. It was Thunderheart who had taught him to fish during those glorious golden days of his first summer. But now she was gone, as was Faolan's first Milk Giver. He chewed the fish head and looked up toward the sky. It had started to snow again. He turned his face toward the constellations of the Cave of Souls and Ursulana, the wolf and the bear heavens. It didn't matter that he could not see the stars. He knew that both his Milk Givers were up there, snug in their heavens.

The wind had picked up and was cutting down from the north like a blade. To head directly into it for the Ring would be hard going, especially on their meager meal of three scrawny fish.

"All right," Faolan sighed. "With this wind we'd do better tacking across instead of facing it straight on. We'll head toward the eastern edges of the MacNab and the MacDuff territories. Let's go."

The snow stopped as they left the Shadow Forest behind. There were drifts on the ground, but they were not too thick and Faolan and Edme were able to increase their speed considerably. The sun rode high in the sky, beating down fiercely on them and threatening to put an icy glaze on the trail, which would make it even more difficult for them. Edme was thinking about the irony of the summer sun and the threat of ice occurring simultaneously. *How can a world turn so strange so quickly?* she thought as she trotted along several paces behind Faolan. Suddenly, she saw Faolan skid to a halt. "Not already!" she muttered and accelerated her pace to catch up. She was careful to lock her toes into the snow to avoid skidding.

"Look ahead!" It had begun to snow again, hard. A driving wind flung the swirling gusts smack into their faces, but something else came on the edge of those gusts — a scent. The scent of meat. The snowflakes seemed to freeze in place. The wind stopped and a shadow loomed dark behind the white veil of the blizzard. It was a moose.

The tang of the animal's meat saturated the air. Could they take down one of the largest animals in the Beyond? This one didn't look full-grown, but it still could be dangerous. Moose were unpredictable and many a wolf had died after being charged and then impaled on the sharp rack of their antlers.

Faolan's and Edme's stomachs churned. A new energy flooded through them and both sprang in a dead run downwind of the moose until he was within kill range. There was no way they were going to let the creature pick up their scent.

Now! Faolan signaled silently with a flick of his ears. He split off from Edme, heading upwind. Edme tore through the blizzard at such a speed that she left a wake in the wind-driven snow, a narrow path that seemed fragrant with the smell of meat. Within seconds, the moose caught her scent and began to run. He was small for a moose, but he was fast. Faolan drove down on his port flank, trying to turn the moose in a classic outflanker maneuver. Meanwhile, Edme was packing the gap. *Is she packing already?* Faolan wondered. This was risky. The moose was turning too sharply.

"Let it go!" Faolan howled the cease chase call. His eyes widened in horror. Edme was not stopping. The moose caught a glimpse of Edme out of one eye and let out a bellow that shook the blizzarding sky. He was going to turn and charge.

"Edme!" Faolan cried. He saw something small fly through the air. And then everything stopped for him, everything except the echo of the bellowing moose as it hammered away into what was now a blinding blizzard.

"Edme?" Faolan looked around desperately. The bellows of the moose began to diminish with the distance. "Edme?" His voice cracked.

He saw something stir in a small drift ahead.

"I'm all right. I'm fine," Edme said as she emerged from a mound of snow. She wobbled slightly, but Faolan could see no blood.

"Edme, wh . . . what . . ." Faolan could barely form the question. "Why would you do such a thing? That was *cag mag*! To make a move like that, to cut in." His eyes darkened with disbelief.

"I know . . . I mean, I know now. But all I could think of was meat. It was scary. Or it's scary now to think that I did this. I was just so hungry." She looked at Faolan. He was shaking.

"Edme, if he had killed you . . . if . . ."

"I didn't mean to fighten you, Faolan." She was suddenly filled with a terrible sadness. She came up to Faolan and nuzzled his shoulder. "I'm here, Faolan. I'm just fine. I'll never do anything like that again."

"Do you promise?"

Edme was silent for several seconds. "I was driven by an urge that made me senseless. Even a sensible wolf can lose her mind. I won't let it ever happen again. I promise." She paused. "But I did learn one thing."

"What was that?"

"Faolan, I got so close to that moose I could smell milk on him — old milk."

"Old milk? You mean . . ."

"I mean that was a calf moose. He should have been with his mum. They always stay with their mums to nurse until the first of the snow moons. You know that."

"His mum must be dead," Faolan said.

"If that happened, usually another moose cow would have taken on the orphan, like a second Milk Giver."

"In other words, this might be the last moose in the Beyond." This was not a question, but a statement.

CHAPTER FOUR

SECRETS OF THE *GADDERHEAL*

FAOLAN AND EDME WERE EXHAUSTED by the time they entered the Ring of Sacred Volcanoes. They immediately headed toward the den they shared near the volcano known as Stormfast.

"Uh-oh, guess who's coming." Edme sighed. Faolan didn't even have to look to know who Edme was talking about. It was Banja, the red wolf who seemed to take a special delight in tormenting Edme. Banja, like Edme, was missing one eye. But sharing the same deformity didn't make her empathetic in the least. Sometimes Faolan got so angry at the bitter she-wolf that he felt like body-slamming her.

"You two will be late for your shift," Banja growled. "We need all the wolves possible. Too many cairns are untopped."

Cairns of bones had been constructed to look out on the five volcanoes of the Ring. On top of each one, a wolf perched to guard the powerful Ember of Hoole and protect it from graymalkins, the treacherous owls who might attempt to seize it. This task, regarded as a sacred one, had been entrusted to the wolves by the owls of the Great Ga'Hoole Tree over one thousand years before. The balance of not just the Beyond but of the entire Hoolian empire depended on this trust. The ember must never fall into the talons of a traitorous owl. But as the hunger moons of winter stretched into the summer, Watch wolves had been called upon to go out to scout for meat. With an incomplete Watch, cairns were often left "untopped."

Colleen, an earless silver wolf, was passing and caught the edge of Banja's rant.

"Banja, don't be ridiculous. For Lupus' sake, these two have been out on scout for four days. They need to rest, but even before they rest, the Fengo would like to see them in the *gadderheal*."

"What? They are being called to the *gadderheal?*" Banja seemed stunned. "But the *raghnaid* is about to meet. I was on my way there."

"As I am myself," Colleen replied coolly.

"But young wolves never attend *raghnaid* meetings. It's an offense."

"An offense to what?" Colleen pressed.

"An offense to . . . to . . ." Banja stammered. "To the order."

Colleen, ever patient, tipped her head to one side. "Banja, these are difficult times. We are being stressed in ways we'd never imagined before."

"Therefore the order needs to be maintained."

"The spirit of the order will be maintained. It is the spirit that keeps the codes and laws of the Beyond alive." Colleen turned to Faolan and Edme. "Now come, you two. The Fengo is waiting."

As they entered the *gadderheal*, Finbar, Fengo of the Watch, rose from the pelts on which he had been resting.

"Welcome, Faolan and Edme. Do you have any news of the herds?"

"No good news, I'm afraid," Edme replied softly. She briefly described the prints from the caribou herd that seemed to circle endlessly and then inexplicably vanish.

"Disturbing, very disturbing," the Fengo murmured. "So they are trying to migrate along their usual trails, but somehow lose their way."

"Yes, sir. So it seems. But there is something even more disturbing."

"More disturbing?" the Fengo asked, and shoved his ears forward.

Together, Edme and Faolan described their encounter with the young moose. By the time they concluded, a thick silence had fallen upon the *gadderheal*. Finally, the Fengo cocked his head to one side and whispered into the dimness of the cave. "Old milk. Old milk," he repeated, then simply shook his head in wonder. "And not a sign of a bull or cow around, you say?"

Edme and Faolan both nodded.

"No sign, sir," Faolan added.

"Did you find any other game at all? How did you manage a four-day scout with nothing to eat?" Banja asked in an accusatory tone.

Faolan glared at the red wolf. "The same way the other scouts did, I imagine — on the occasional snow hare and three fish that we broke through creek ice for."

"Please, let us set such trifling questions and explanations aside," the Fengo said, nodding at both Faolan and Banja. Edme had not been paying much attention to this exchange. She was scanning the cave for Winks, her *taiga*, but there was no sign of the brown one-eyed wolf. She often wondered how Banja and Winks, two wolves who had both been born with only one eye, could be so different.

"I've called this meeting because we have had some disturbing reports from the MacDuncan clan. You may recall that Cathmor MacDuncan, mate of the late Duncan MacDuncan, has gone the way of the star ladder. She was safely guided by Skaarsgard and blessed that it was the time of the Great Wolf constellation."

There were murmurs of agreement from the assembled wolves.

" 'Twas a blessing indeed," Twist said.

"Aye," said another wolf.

"Now a new report has just reached us," the Fengo continued.

A current of tension ran through the *gadderheal* as ruffs bristled and wolves shoved their ears forward in sharp attention.

"We have always known that Liam, the son of Duncan MacDuncan and Cathmor, is not the strongest leader. He has now sunk into a deep depression and has begun to wander off for long periods of time. The MacDuncans are being stressed in ways that go beyond hunger. We have even heard rumors that a MacDuncan wolf has been charged with a willful attack on a

MacAngus wolf over meat. The MacAngus wolf died from its wounds."

Yips erupted from the small group of wolves. Faolan shut his eyes and imagined drops of blood falling from the sky instead of snow.

It was unthinkable that a MacDuncan would do such a thing.

"Wolves are beginning to starve, and now we have this. It is my feeling that the leadership in the clan has broken down." The Fengo lowered his voice. "And, worse, the Blood Watch has been compromised." A shiver ran through both Faolan and Edme. The outclanners were the most savage of all wolves, and the Blood Watch ensured that they stayed safely away in the Outermost. If outclanners dared to venture over the border into the Beyond, they were killed immediately. Within the clans of the Beyond, certain wolves were selected very young to train for the Blood Watch. It was a hard post, and they were rotated out of the Watch every moon cycle. Their task was so vital that there were usually plenty of reserves to maintain the Blood Watch.

"Blood Watch wolves have gone *by-lang*," the Fengo continued.

The *taigas* Malachy and Twist shook their heads

wearily. For a Blood Watch wolf to wander off was unthinkable.

"Edme and Faolan, once you are rested, your first order of business is to go directly to the MacDuncans. Find out what in the name of the dim world is going on with that clan. Then go on to the Blood Watch. And if it is true that they are in a bad way, try and fix the situation. Get more wolves. Stay yourselves, if you have to. The clan chieftain should be in charge of organizing the Blood Watch. But, as I said, we get reports that Liam himself is inclined to go *by-lang* and disappear for days on end. He can't send out the rotations if he's not there. Do you understand your mission?"

Faolan and Edme both nodded solemnly.

"Good. Then neither of you is to report for watch this evening."

The Fengo nodded that the meeting of the *gadderheal* was finished.

As the last of the wolves left the *gadderheal*, the Fengo motioned for Edme to wait. "Edme, I saw you looking for your dear *taiga*, Winks."

Edme's jaw began to quiver.

"Winks is quite ill. You know she is the oldest of the Watch wolves. She served in the time before the Fengo

Hamish. But she is weak now. She could use some good meat, of which there is precious little. But I am not sure even that would cure her. Lupus knows if she will last until you return."

Edme tried to look brave. She tried not to whimper. Her eye filmed with tears as she began to speak. "Winks and Twist were Faolan's and my first friends on the Watch. They greeted us at the Hot Gates and taught us everything they know. They are both the best *taigas* a Watch wolf could ever have."

"I know, I know," the Fengo whispered. "This is difficult for you. I can remember when my *taiga* went the way of the star ladder. *Taigas* are the closest we Watch wolves have to a mother or father." The Fengo paused. "But you are strong, Edme. You are smaller perhaps than your friend Faolan, but just as strong in spirit. After you have visited Winks, go join Faolan in your den and both of you rest. I have arranged to have some food — not much, mind you — delivered to you. Eat, rest, then on the morrow, set off."

CHAPTER FIVE

The Inner Eye

"HAS IT OCCURRED TO YOU," Winks asked Edme in a raspy voice, "that with one eye we often see more than those with two?"

Edme could barely stand to look at her dear old *taiga*. Winks's once lustrous brown pelt had turned almost white in the short time Edme had been gone. It made her think of that moment when Faolan had appeared in their scouting cave, covered in frost and snow. She had taken him for the ghost of a very old wolf. But while Faolan had loomed large and radiant although ancient, Winks seemed nothing more than a pile of bones, a sort of living cairn. It made Edme shiver to even compare her beloved *taiga* to such, for the cairns were made from the bones of Watch wolves and other animals. And Winks seemed a hairbreadth away from joining them.

"I don't know. I'm not sure if Banja sees that much with her one eye," Edme replied.

"Oh, Banja! Don't pay her any heed."

Edme was about to sigh and say it was hard not to, but caught herself in time. How could she whine to this beloved wolf? Edme had brought Winks some meat, but Winks said that she was not hungry. Edme felt death crouching like a dark shadow in the cave. "Are you sure you aren't hungry, Winks? I've got some nice ptarmigan here for you."

"No, not at all, dear," Winks whispered. "Not hungry in the least."

"Are you cold, then? Let me get you another pelt."

A sudden energy seemed to course through the old wolf, and she slapped her paw onto Edme's with surprising force.

"Listen to me, young'un. I sense that you do see things."

"What kinds of things?" Edme asked.

"When you came in here, there was shock in your eye when you saw my pelt — all white now. But you weren't upset simply by my transformation. I think I reminded you of something. Something or someone that has disturbed you."

Winks was right. Edme had been haunted by the vision of Faolan ever since they had left the Shadow Forest.

"I am not one to pry," Winks continued. "You need not tell me. I only ask you to open that intelligent eye of yours and ponder." She weakly lifted her paw and tapped her face near the eye. "I sometimes call this my outside eye, and on occasion it seems to connect with an inner eye, an eye deep inside my head, a kind of spirit eye. Together they guide me. That is what guided me back to the MacDonegals when I was a pup on a *tummfraw*. I know you are to go to the Blood Watch to check on the border guard. Finbar told me of the mission. So I am just saying be alert, be aware that the eye on your face is not the only eye you possess, my dear. Now run along and get your rest."

Winks sighed deeply. The talk had worn her out. Edme crouched down closer to her old *taiga* to nuzzle her ruff before she left. She was shocked to see how thin Winks's undercoat was. In this never-ending cold, most wolves had kept their thick winter fur, but Winks's undercoat was as thin as if it were a warm summer. Edme got up and pulled another caribou pelt over her friend. She did not want to say good-bye. She did not want to utter those two dead-sounding words. She turned to look at her *taiga.*

"It's never good-bye, Edme," said Winks. "It's merely *slaan boladh.*"

"*Slaan boladh?*" Edme repeated.

"Old Wolf for 'until the next scent post.'"

"*Slaan boladh,*" Edme murmured, and turned and left her *taiga* to sleep.

By the time Edme returned to the den, Faolan was already asleep. She collapsed on a caribou pelt beside him and fell into a deep sleep, entering a dreamscape of swirling mists. The frost wolf that Edme had seen in the den near the Shadow Forest began to wander through the dream rivers in her mind.

Who are you? *Edme heard her dream self asking.*

Who are you? You have two eyes, *the frost wolf replied.* But I only see one.

And Edme answered: I have eyes enough to see you, to see through you to what you already know. The snow is dissolving. I see you in another pelt — a pelt within a pelt.

You speak nonsense, *the frost wolf answered.*

The inner eye of Edme blinked. It's not nonsense, Faolan. *She began to see something more. A wind riffled the pelt. Where there had been fur, feathers rose, mottled with flakes as white as snow. Green eyes turned a yellow that was as bright as gold.*

My name is not Faolan.

Edme's inner eye blinked. You're right. Your name is not Faolan. *Edme was riveted by the transformation occurring in front of her. The creature was standing at the mouth of a cave that seemed to yawn out of the mists, its darkness beckoning. She watched as it drew nearer to the opening.*

Who am I? *the creature asked desperately. The Spotted Owl that moments before had been a frost wolf began to melt away, dissolving into the shadows of the cave.*

"Wake up, Edme. Wake up! We're half past moonrise. We need to be on our way."

Edme's eyes flew open. Faolan was nudging her with his muzzle to rouse her. She stood up.

"Sleep well, Faolan?" she asked.

"Oh, yes, and you?"

"Yes. Very deeply."

Edme remembered nothing, not even the slightest wisp of a dream.

CHAPTER SIX

Most Foul!

THE SLOUGH TERN WAS THE ONLY bird in the Beyond that laid its eggs underground. It buried them in earliest spring and awaited their hatching in the Moon of the Flies. But the Moon of the Flies had come and gone, as had the parents of the clutch of eggs. The eggs were not going to hatch. And so the Sark of the Slough did not feel too bad when she decided to dig them up for food.

This had not been as hard as one might imagine, for though the marshy ground of the Slough was frozen solid, the Sark had transported some coals from her kiln to thaw the spot where she knew the eggs were buried. Once the ground had softened from the heat, she dug in and extracted two eggs.

Several hours later, the Sark of the Slough belched and reflected that she probably should not have eaten the eggs. *As if I am not disgusting enough*, the Sark thought as she got a whiff of her own recent digestive activities. Her blighted eye, given to skittish twirls, spun madly as she tried to suppress another belch. Her one normal eye wept cold tears that quickly froze on her muzzle, hanging like a second set of fangs. Her fur, always in disarray, was shingled with icicles.

The Sark had spent most of her time recently near her kiln and was relatively warm. When she had ventured out on brief forays into the cold, she rarely built up quite enough snow to form icicles. But the fires in her kiln had dwindled as the herds had moved off to Lupus knew where. The Sark depended on their droppings for fuel.

On this particular day, the Sark had gone to her favorite perch on an escarpment to survey the Slough and see if she could spot any herds in the distance. Her stomach rumbled with the memory of meat. Real meat!

Normally at this time of year, three herds had passed through the Slough with the Blue Rock Pack of the MacDuncan clan hard on their heels. The marshy land clicked with the *tock-tock* of the caribou's march across the Beyond, a distinctive clicking sound made by the caribous' tendons. The wolves formed hunting *byrrgises* and kept after the caribou at a steady speed, known as tock-tock pace, until they could identify a weak member of the herd and take it down.

The Sark often joined the *byrrgis*, taking any position she was assigned and then receiving her share of the kill. But so far, only one small herd had come through. Two packs of the MacDuncan clan had joined together for the hunt, the Blue Rock Pack and the chieftain's pack, the Carreg Gaer. It had not gone well. The *byrrgises* of the two packs argued the entire time. Liam MacDuncan, the new chieftain, was running as a turning guard, but leadership was decidedly absent. The Sark had been running on the opposite side of the *byrrgis*, waiting for the chieftain's signal to begin packing the herd. Janna, the Blue Rock tight end packer, kept glancing the Sark's way to see if she had received a sign. But Liam was hesitant in his signaling. He would begin to signal, then stop midway, as if he couldn't quite make a decision. A line wolf, key to the passing of signals, stumbled and became so frustrated that he actually yipped out a signal, even though signals were never called out loud except to order a cease chase. At that point everything began to crumble. Wolves bumped up against one another, snapping and nipping. Within a matter of seconds, the *byrrgis* had disintegrated into utter chaos. The Sark broke away and watched the collapse in a kind of horrified fascination.

It had pained her to see this happening, for a *byrrgis* was usually a beautiful thing. Signals were passed flawlessly to alter pace, sometimes racing to attack speed, other times shifting to press-paw speed or slowing even further to deceive the herd that the wolves were wearing out. There was a silent splendor about the endeavor, an unmatched grace as the wolves wove in and out of their positions to maneuver the herd and isolate its weakest member to bring it down for the kill. It took cunning, cooperation, and perfect communication.

The *byrrgis* — no matter how many wolves — always moved as one. Individuals were absorbed into a fluid whole. Pelts blended into a subtly hued wave of fur curling across the vastness of the waterless sea known as the Beyond. And in a night of boisterous winds, with the sky torn by racing clouds, the moon might shine down to cast a devilish brilliance upon their pelts. The shadow of the *byrrgis* slid across the hard land like a ghost ship. The wolves' lungs merged into one immense pumping bellows. Separate hearts became one huge beating organ. The wolves' marrows fused into a single mighty river. There was a splendid unity to it all. It was a sight that greatly amazed the Sark, and there was nothing like it in the Beyond. No other animals could do what wolf packs did when they ran together on a hunt.

After Liam MacDuncan's *byrrgis* had fallen apart, the Sark heard nothing but snarling wolves tackling one another and barking recriminations. The Sark's skittering eye had twirled in mad disbelief. Driven by sheer hunger, these wolves had become absolutely despicable. In her long life, the Sark had observed more *byrrgises* than perhaps any other wolf in the Beyond. What she saw that day almost shattered her. She understood — better than any wolf — that a *byrrgis* was a microcosm of the whole wolf world and its clan system. The wolves depended on decisive communication. A leader, whether a clan chieftain or a turning guard, had to have strength of conviction to make decisions. That's what the *byrrgis* needed and that's what a clan needed. It was how a leader earned respect and could command. Without respect, discipline dissolved like morning fog in a noon sun. And that was precisely what had happened with the *byrrgis* that the Sark had joined a half moon before. The Sark would never forget the image of Liam MacDuncan slinking off after the humiliating failure of the hunt.

Normally, the Sark, known for her extraordinary sense of smell, would sniff out herds before she could spot them. But with the baffling weather of late, the winds had switched and she would never catch a whiff of caribou with the way it was blowing. Indeed, it was more likely that the herd would catch her scent — the stench of the two rotten Slough tern eggs — before she could smell them. However, she could see something glinting enigmatically in the distance. It wasn't a low-setting sun, for the sky was shrouded in thick dark clouds. But from close to the ground came a metallic shimmer. Then she caught sight of some animals. Although they were blurry, they looked like wolves. Her sight was not as good as her sense of smell. "Calm down," she quietly ordered her skittish eye. "For Lupus' sake, let me see. Got to draw a bead on this." *They look like wolves but they don't move like wolves*, she thought. She decided to creep down the escarpment. It wasn't far to another ridge where she could get a better look.

Despite the wind carrying their howls away, she could hear the wolves distinctly now. But their wailing made no sense. "The Prophet . . . the Prophet . . . and in my sacred pelt I shall dance to the place of warmth and meat and everlasting game. . . ."

Sacred pelt! she thought. *They look more like bags of bones.* There were a dozen or more wolves dancing in a circle and crying out for a prophet. They appeared weak, and exhausted to the point that some of them were collapsing.

Suddenly, the glint that the Sark had spied from afar flashed from the center of the circle. A creature rose up wearing a mask, a visor of metal that was fixed to a helmet. The creature was the size of a wolf. It had the legs of a wolf but was like no wolf the Sark had ever seen.

She caught the glint of the visor straight in her bad eye, which set it spinning again. She clapped a paw over it for several seconds, as if the eye were a naughty pup trying to escape the whelping den. "Behave yourself," she growled. Then slowly she removed her paw. She could see clearly now and she could hear clearly. In another few seconds, the wind shifted and she could smell as well.

"A MacDuff, at least two MacNabs," she whispered to herself. But the thing that shocked the Sark the most was the creature in the metal visor. The wind had shifted and brought a scent, but it was indecipherable, for mingled with it was more than a trace of owl. *Corrupt!* the Sark thought. But it was not simply the smell that was corrupt. It was the dance and what these wolves were howling. The wind blew harder and a new scent came to her. *Dream marks! How could they?* Dream marks were special scent signs left to indicate a place where a mate had died or a pup was lost. Were the wolves dancing on someone's grave? *It might as well be their own*, thought the Sark as she watched them limp off into the distance.

"This is most foul!" she muttered. And with that, the Sark vomited up the eggs she had eaten that morning.

CHAPTER SEVEN

FRAYED TEMPERS

AN OWL MESSENGER HAD BEEN sent from the Ring to the Carreg Gaer of the MacDuncan clan to inform them that two Watch wolves would be arriving. This was not good news for Liam MacDuncan. Word of the disastrous two-pack *byrrgis* must have reached the Fengo. For emissaries to be sent to interfere with the business of the Carreg Gaer was one more threat to his authority. This never would have happened in his father's time, and his *raghnaid* would be the first to remind him of that. Now he was going to have to break the news to the *raghnaid* and other high-ranking wolves of the clan who had assembled in the *gadderheal.* How would he put it? More important, how would his mother, Cathmor, have put it? Liam's eyes began to fill with tears. *Don't cry!* he admonished himself. *Whatever you do, don't cry.*

Liam MacDuncan realized that it was silly of him to try to guess what his mother might say in this situation, because had she not died, agents from the Ring would never be coming. She would have managed to govern the clan through these terrible times.

Why? Why did she have to die and leave me with this mess? If his parents had only let him do more when he was younger, be more independent, he'd know what to do now. *No . . . no!* he scolded himself. He shouldn't blame his parents; they had tried their best. His eyes filled again with tears. Liam MacDuncan, young chieftain of the MacDuncan clan, was caught in an endless cycle of shame and rage.

He looked into the dim light of the *gadderheal.* Perhaps he would delay sharing the news for one more day. *Yes, that's it! I'll call for the* skreeleen.

"Uh . . . uh . . ." he began nervously. "Is Alastrine here?" he asked tentatively.

"Alastrine?!" asked Lord Adair. "Whatcha want with her, Li — I mean, honorable chieftain?" He nearly choked on the last two words.

Liam MacDuncan squared his shoulders and tried to assume an authoritative posture. "It might interest you to know, Lord Adair, that I would like her to consult with the wind scouts."

"Wind scouts!" someone shouted. "Why in the name of Lupus would you call for the wind scouts?"

"For any storms," Liam snapped.

"Ain't we got enough?" someone barked from the back. There was an explosion of laughter.

"I wasn't . . . talking about bl . . . bl . . ." he stammered. "Blizzards! I was talking about rainstorms, *ceilidh fyre*, sky fire. We have the best *skreeleen* in the Beyond. She can read the sky fire of summer storms as no one else and give us guidance."

"It might be summer, but these ain't summer storms," howled the wolf in the back.

"Don't talk to our chieftain in that manner!" someone else snarled.

Outside, Mhairie the young outflanker and her sister Dearlea tried their best to hear what was going on inside the *gadderheal* cave.

"They're fighting again," Dearlea said.

"What else is new?" Mhairie replied with a sigh. "Everything is wrong, just plain wrong. Upside down and backward."

"That fool chieftain!" Mhairie muttered. "Lord Adair is absolutely bamboozling him. Nobody understands it, not even the *raghnaid*."

"There are rumors that the Watch is sending some wolves to see what is happening," Dearlea said grimly.

"Nothing is happening. That is the problem. How long has it been since the last rotation for the Blood Watch? How long has Mum been gone on the Blood Watch — two moons? She should have been back by now." Mhairie paused, her tail drooping. "Maybe she feels that she has nothing to come back to since Da died."

"She has the pups."

"The pups aren't pups anymore. They're almost as grown up as we are."

"Well, then she has us and the almost grown-up pups."

Mhairie sighed. "I don't know."

"What do you mean you don't know?" Dearlea asked.

"I think Mum doesn't like an empty den. Ever since I can remember, she had a litter every spring. She gave birth to more pups than any female in the clan."

"But the pups are still here even if they aren't pups anymore. We're still here," Dearlea replied stubbornly.

"Sometimes I wonder if she felt the same way about us as she did the pups," Mhairie whispered.

"Have you gone *cag mag*? Of course she did. She appreciated how much we helped her with the pups since we were the oldest. And tell me who in the world would choose to go on the Blood Watch if they didn't have to? I don't think she's staying out there just for her own amusement, Mhairie."

"Maybe she found a new mate. Someone else to have pups with."

"I'm not going to listen to another thing you say. You're just being completely foolish." And to emphasize her point, Dearlea gave her sister a quick body slam.

"Ouch!" Mhairie yelped. "Neither one of us has enough meat on our bones for that." Indeed, the impact had jolted both their bones. This struck them as oddly funny, and they began to laugh and tussle. They were both laughing hard when they heard a familiar voice.

"Well, I'm glad someone around here has found something to laugh about."

The two she-wolves disentangled themselves and leaped up from the ground. "Faolan! Edme!"

"So it's true?" Dearlea said.

"What's true?" Edme asked.

"There were rumors that the Fengo was sending wolves to check on us."

"Yes, and from the sound of it, something is going on inside." Edme tipped her head toward the *gadderheal.*

"It's always like that," Mhairie sighed. "They fight all the time."

"Is the chieftain in there?" Faolan asked.

"Yes," Dearlea said.

"Is it true that the chieftain wanders off?" Edme asked.

"Yes, every now and then. And then he wanders back," Mhairie answered.

Faolan took a step closer to Mhairie. He had not seen either one of the sister wolves for a while. There was always something that fascinated him about their eyes, especially now. And oddly enough, as the two she-wolves stared back at him, each felt a slight stirring in their marrow. What was it about him? Why had they wanted to protect him when he was still a gnaw wolf?

"So what's going on in there?" Edme asked. "What are they arguing about?"

"They seem to be arguing about finding Alastrine," Mhairie said.

"Alastrine — your *skreeleen*? Why?" Faolan asked.

Wearily, Mhairie began to explain. "Liam wants her to consult with wind scouts. He's hoping for a storm, not a blizzard."

"He wants her to read the *ceilidh fyre*?" Faolan asked in disbelief.

"Yes," Mhairie answered. "He can't make up his own mind what to do. His mum isn't around anymore to do it for him. So he looks to the sky. But he'd do a better job looking to the Blood Watch."

"What do you mean?" Edme asked.

"The Blood Watch hasn't changed in over a moon," Dearlea explained.

Edme and Faolan exchanged glances. So what the Fengo had told them was true. The Blood Watch was unstable.

Dearlea continued. "The same blooders are still at the border. No new wolves have been sent."

"Our mum's been gone since the end of the Moon of New Antlers." Mhairie paused. Her voice cracked a bit when she began to speak. "We miss her."

"How long has it been this way? The disorder, the arguing?" Edme asked, nodding toward the *gadderheal*.

"Since Cathmor died. First, Liam sank into this terrible grief. It was after that, I think, that he started wandering off. As if he didn't care anymore. And he just wasn't able to make decisions about anything. When he's here, it's not exactly like he's still grieving, but he's not himself. That's the best way I can put it," Dearlea said.

"I think we need to find Caila. We need to find your

mum," Faolan said grimly. "And I think we need to find the rest of your clan's blooders."

Faolan and Edme turned toward the cave opening. The tumult inside had grown louder. The two wolves looked at each other. Resolutely they entered the din and darkness of the *gadderheal*, their tails high, their ears shoved forward.

CHAPTER EIGHT

A *RAGHNAID* IN SHAMBLES

AS THEY ENTERED THE CAVE, FAOLAN looked around. *Why are the enormous caribou antlers slightly askew?* he wondered. Beneath the antlers, the chieftain sat on a pile of pelts, his own ceremonial headdress tipped at an odd angle. These were two slight irregularities that should not mean anything, and yet they were the first things that Faolan noticed. How different everything seemed now that Cathmor was gone. The fire in the center pit was sputtering because no one had bothered to tend it. Many of the *raghnaid* members were not wearing the headdresses or bone necklaces that were required when a session was called. But was this a session? Some wolves seemed to be sleeping, oblivious to the din around them. All of them looked extremely thin, and their pelts were far from lustrous. But then again, the

Watch wolves had grown thinner as well, their coats duller. *Yet*, thought Faolan, *we still hold ourselves with dignity*.

That was it, he realized — the decorum, the dignity, and the solemnity of the *gadderheal* had vanished. The props were still there. The beautifully carved bones that generations of gnaw wolves had incised still gleamed with their intricate designs. The pelts of animals brought down in *byrrgises* still hung from stone pegs, many turned inside out and decorated with designs etched from charred wood. But the artifacts of death seemed more expressive of this venerable clan's majesty than the clan wolves themselves. There was nothing noble, nothing dignified, and not a trace of majesty left in this *gadderheal* that had once inspired a gnaw wolf to seek a righteous life and honor bones with his finest carving.

Even the beautifully incised bones seemed to mutter with despair. Deep in his marrow, Faolan felt an ache for what had been. He looked over at Liam MacDuncan, who seemed confused by the squabbling among the lords of the *raghnaid*. Occasionally, he got up from his special pelts beneath the massive caribou antlers and circled nervously. His eyes glistened with anxiety, as if he were on the brink of tears. As he circled, he lifted each paw high and hesitated, almost as though he were testing the firmness of this sovereign ground.

It took several seconds for the wolves in the *gadderheal* to realize that Faolan and Edme had entered. But when they did, an immediate hush fell in the cave.

"What are you doing here?" Lord Jarne roared. His ears had not lain back or even twitched. Such insolence to a Watch wolf from the Ring of Sacred Volcanoes was unheard of.

Faolan and Edme shoved their ears up and walked forward on stiff legs with their tails raised and their hackles bristling. Faolan came so close to the insolent Lord Jarne that their noses almost touched.

"I come by direct command of the Fengo of the Watch of the Ring of Sacred Volcanoes." It was as if every wolf in the cave were holding its breath. "We have come to inquire about the rotations of the Blood Watch."

Liam felt his knees grow weak.

"Why didn't you tell us that the Fengo was sending Watch wolves, Liam?" someone barked from the back. Edme and Faolan were shocked. The wolves were not even using the proper form of address for their chieftain. This was another appalling breach of etiquette.

"Yes, why not?"

"Why not?"

Soon there was a chorus of howling wolves, and the cave teetered on the brink of chaos. Edme shot Faolan a desperate glance.

As if lifted up by his own anger, Faolan rose on his hind legs and began to walk above the crowd. Thunderheart had taught him to do this. When Faolan had jumped the wall of fire as a yearling, wolves had been stunned, but this was entirely different. Jumping, even jumping high, was in the range of moves of a wolf, but walking on hind legs was an extraordinary endeavor, a feat. The light from the small fire burning in the pit in the middle of the *gadderheal* cast Faolan's shadow against the rock walls of the cave, and his dark profile seemed to stretch endlessly. All the wolves began to cower, and even Jarne and Adair assumed the most extreme of submission postures. *Good!* Faolan always knew those two lords were idiots and decided not to waste another second with them. But then another wolf rose and began to snarl.

"You know nothing! And how do we know you have been officially sent by the Fengo? If our chieftain didn't tell us, perhaps it was because your visit is not sanctioned at all."

The two lords whom Faolan had just decided not to waste time on began to rise up. Faolan's and Edme's instincts were perfectly in sync. In tandem, they leaped forward, Edme body-checking the wolf who had snarled, and Faolan kicking down Jarne and Adair. But it was the cold hard look in Faolan's eyes more than anything else that vanquished the two lords. Their marrow froze.

"It matters not what the chieftain did or did not tell you," Faolan roared. He turned again to Liam. "What matters now is for you to stand forward, Liam MacDuncan, son of Duncan MacDuncan, great chieftain of the MacDuncan clan, and son of Cathmor, noble she-wolf, renowned turning guard. You are the grandson of Dunforth MacDuncan, great-grandson of the first Liam MacDuncan, and descended from MacDuncans stretching back to the time of the first Fengo of the Beyond!"

With each name that was called out, Liam shrank farther into his pelt until he seemed as small, insubstantial, and frail as a wolf four times his age. An immutable silence suffused the cave. Every wolf had its eyes fastened on their chieftain as if trying to imagine his illustrious predecessors. *Yes,* thought Faolan, *think of your history. Think of the honor of this clan since the time the first Fengo arrived in the Beyond. If we forget, we shall fall, and if we fall, then the whole Beyond will fall as well, and we shall sink into an abyss of darkness.*

The words came to Faolan, but he did not know from where. He dared not speak them aloud. It was as if he were in a *byrrgis* and the signals all had to be passed in silence until the barks of cease chase were howled. He looked hard at the wolves assembled around him and hoped they saw something in his eyes that was more urgent than words.

"As chieftain of this clan," Faolan continued, "you need to answer an important question. When was your last rotation of the Blood Watch?"

"I . . . I . . . I'm not sure."

"Not sure?" Edme stepped forward. The chieftain was trembling so hard he could barely answer. "Try to remember."

"Maybe at the beginning of the New Antlers' Moon?"

"Maybe, just maybe?" Edme asked. Faolan and Edme looked at each other in dismay.

There was a disturbance at the mouth of the cave. Alastrine, the *skreeleen* of the Carreg Gaer, made her way in.

"The Blood Watch wolves have not been rotated for almost two moons. Some have come back, such as Stellan, though they were not called. We thank Lupus she did come back, for she is our best outflanker. But Caila has not returned."

"She ain't been much of a point wolf since her mate jumped the star ladder," someone called out from the back of the cave.

"Shame on you!" Alastrine charged the wolf. "Is that the way to speak of a wolf's passing? This is profane!"

Faolan and Edme were shocked as well, but Alastrine kindled a spark of hope within them. At last a rational wolf with a sense of dignity!

But their question had been answered — answered in a way that they dreaded reporting to the Fengo. They must leave immediately to follow the Fengo's command and shore up the Blood Watch. Faolan decided to take Mhairie and Dearlea with them. The thought of leaving the two sisters with the MacDuncan clan in its present state was abhorrent. They would all travel together to the Blood Watch and find the sisters' mother, Caila. But before they left, Faolan announced to the wolves assembled in the *gadderheal* that, by the full authority granted him by the Fengo, he was appointing Alastrine first lieutenant to the chieftain in place of Lord Adair. Liam MacDuncan looked profoundly relieved.

CHAPTER NINE

THE FIRST SIGN

FAOLAN'S THOUGHTS BRIMMED with memories of Thunderheart as he set out with Edme, Mhairie, and Dearlea through the slashing wind toward the border and the Blood Watch. A northwest wind was blowing and the gusts slammed squarely into their faces, making the pace excruciatingly slow. They were traveling almost the same route he had taken when he was just a yearling and had gone in search of his beloved second Milk Giver when she had disappeared from their winter den. He had headed toward the Outermost in hopes of finding her.

However, he had not been as hungry then as he was now.

Since they left the MacDuncan Carreg Gaer, the supply of small game and even the ever-dependable snow hares had dwindled. They had to take more frequent rests, for they simply did not have the energy against this wind. And when they rested, their stomachs rumbled. Edme, who was the smallest of the four, seemed to produce the loudest rumbles. "Truly an example of a bark worse than a bite," she quipped, then sighed. "Aah, for a bite!"

"Remember when we used to think snow hares were slightly disgusting?" Dearlea mused.

"It was just those pinkish eyes. Their meat was fine," Mhairie replied.

"I wouldn't care now if they had bright purple eyes," Dearlea said.

The talk of food scarcities led to other thoughts in Faolan's mind.

"Edme," he said as they trotted along after their most recent rest. "If the herds don't come and even the small game vanishes, there will be famine. And you and I both know who will die first."

Edme halted. Her eye grew immense with anxiety. "The gnaw wolves, of course. They're always the last to eat."

"Yes, and last to eat during a famine means the gnaw wolves get nothing. But there's a way to help the gnaw wolves and help the Blood Watch as well."

Edme stopped in her tracks and turned to Faolan. "Brilliant," she exclaimed.

"I haven't even told you yet."

"You don't need to. I should have thought of it myself. We round up as many of our old gnaw wolf friends as possible and take them with us to the Blood Watch."

"Yes, and there's that new one of the MacDonegal clan — what's his name — Streak?"

"The question is, will the pack lords let them go?" Edme said.

"It's not a question at all. Remember, we are acting on direct orders of the Fengo. The Fengo said to fix the Blood Watch."

Edme blinked. "You're right." She paused. "I never thought of it that way." Edme then turned to speak to Mhairie and Dearlea. "We've made a decision. We want to gather all the gnaw wolves we can and take them to the Blood Watch to fill in."

"That's a brilliant idea!" Mhairie said. "Tamsen from the Blue Rock Pack has been at the Blood Watch almost as long as our mum. If she had been back when we teamed with the Blue Rock *byrrgis*, it wouldn't have been such a catastrophe. Maybe if there are more blooders, she can return to her pack."

With the decision to find gnaw wolves, they altered their course for the MacAngus summer camp, hoping to find the gnaw wolf Tearlach.

The four wolves had not been traveling long when all of a sudden the wind brought an alarming scent, and their hackles rose. It was the smell of a dead wolf, but on its edges was a hauntingly familiar scent.

"Tearlach!" Faolan and Edme both howled at once. They raced forward toward a small mound in the snow.

"Tearlach!" Edme's voice broke as they stared at the earless MacAngus gnaw wolf. She squeezed her single eye shut, but a tear leaked out from it. She gulped. "This seems like a cruel joke, doesn't it." She gulped again to suppress a sob. "Just when we decided to take gnaw wolves to the Blood Watch and give them a real chance in life! We were right — they are the first to die!"

Edme and Faolan huddled together. Dearlea and Mhairie stood slightly apart and shuddered as they looked on. The two Watch wolves seemed to be holding each other up as grief racked them.

"This is the first true sign of famine," Faolan whispered.

The four wolves crept closer to the body of the MacAngus gnaw wolf. They all noticed the same thing.

Tearlach had ground his face into the snow, but not in the normal submission posture for a gnaw wolf.

"It's as if he's listening for something," Edme said.

"Listening to the earth beneath the snow and crust of ice," Faolan said, looking down at the jutting bones of the starved wolf.

"But what could he possibly hear? He's earless," Dearlea said.

Faolan and Edme looked up. Both the sisters seemed confounded. What neither one understood — for how could they, being sound wolves not cursed to live without ears or eyes or with a splayed paw — was that a gnaw wolf's flaws often became its strengths. Had not the Fengo himself said at the *gaddergnaw* that Edme's eye guided her like a spirit from the Cave of Souls? And Faolan, despite his splayed paw, ran faster and could jump higher than any other wolf. Tearlach was no exception. Despite his missing ears, he had always been the one to overhear conversations, especially those not meant for gnaw wolves. Now they could only wonder what he had been listening to. Hearing?

"We better move on, I guess," Dearlea said in a soft voice.

Edme looked at Faolan. "No, not yet." And in the next moment both young wolves crouched down and began a series of intricate submission postures that were both delicate and beautiful. And then they began to bay, bay so mournfully that it brought tears to the two sisters' eyes.

Your tangled body will straighten
Your way shall be swift
With hardly a leap your spirit
Will lift
Heed the call of the Great Wolf
You hear it so bright
Like silver it comes on the darkest night
Away . . . away to the Cave of Souls
And never again will you suffer the rage
You are a gnaw wolf no more
But noble, highborn
And never again shall you suffer the scorn.

"Where did you learn that beautiful song?" Mhairie asked.

It was Faolan and Edme's turn to be confounded. They looked at each other with undisguised astonishment.

"It . . . it . . ." Edme stammered. "It just came to us."

Faolan looked down at the body of Tearlach. "We'd best be on our way. There's not much time left for these poor fellows."

Then out from the swirling snow another figure appeared on a mound, and a painful cry rose up. "Faolan!"

Hope sprouted in Faolan like grass in the Moon of New Antlers. There was such music in that cry, a sonorous clarity like no other wolf's howl. Faolan knew it could be only one animal: the Whistler.

CHAPTER TEN

THE WHISTLER

IF IT WAS POSSIBLE, THE WHISTLER seemed even thinner than Tearlach. There was one furless patch on his hips where bone had actually split the skin. Within seconds of seeing his friends, the Whistler had collapsed and fallen into a delirium. The four wolves had dragged his almost lifeless body to a small cave that most likely had been used as a whelping den. Edme quickly found a family of mice. She had dispatched them with a few sharp bites and was attempting to feed small bits of rodent to the Whistler when Faolan spotted a relatively plump snow hare.

"It's a miracle!" Edme exclaimed when Faolan came back with it.

"Wherever did you find him?" Dearlea asked. "It's our first in days."

"I think Lupus was looking out for the Whistler," Faolan said, and dropped the snow hare.

"Let him drink the blood," Mhairie said. "Is the life artery untorn?"

"Yes, I just crushed his skull."

"Good. This is something our mum taught us."

Deftly, Mhairie punctured the life-pumping artery and, with the first weak spurt, picked it up and pressed it to the Whistler's mouth.

"Now, since its heart has stopped beating, we have to pound on the hare's body to pump the blood into the Whistler," Dearlea said.

It did not take long to exhaust the blood of the snow hare, but it was working. The Whistler opened his eyes, blinked once or twice, then spoke in a ragged sibilance.

"Faolan, remember that buck you brought down when we first met?"

"Of course, old friend."

"Oh, my, how you bore down on that buck. I was pretty hungry back then, too."

It always amazed Faolan that when the Whistler spoke, his voice was a hoarse whistle, but when he howled, it was as melodious as the best *skreeleen*'s.

"Don't talk, Whistler. Save your strength."

"Eat a bit of the meat," Dearlea offered.

"So much for submission rituals," the Whistler croaked. Faolan and Edme looked at each other and rolled their eyes. This was pure Whistler. He somehow managed to be grim and funny at the same time. It was a survival strategy that worked.

"I think," Mhairie said, "that the time for submission rituals is over. We are all gnaw wolves now, like it or not."

Faolan, Edme, and the Whistler looked at her curiously. "What exactly do you mean, Mhairie?" Edme asked.

Dearlea didn't wait for her sister to answer. "I know what she means. You saw the MacDuncans fighting in the *gadderheal.* There is no order. The clans are breaking down. It's becoming each wolf for herself, or so it seems."

"But there has to be some order or else we'll never survive," said Edme.

"Maybe we could skip the gnaw wolf part," the Whistler said sleepily.

"Yes," Mhairie said. Then, looking at each of her fellow travelers, she spoke in a low voice. "Maybe we just have to become a new clan ourselves."

Faolan bristled. "You forget. There is still the Watch

at the Ring of Sacred Volcanoes. It is very much in order, and we are on a mission to go to the Blood Watch. To make sure it still stands and to fix it."

"Blood Watch." The words seemed to rouse the Whistler. "You know Tamsen — she was sent to the Blood Watch, but she's been gone for a moon or more now. I was sent out to find her. I thought I had found her track, but then I picked up another."

The speech had clearly exhausted the Whistler, but Faolan felt he had to ask just one more question. "Whose was that?"

"Tearlach — I thought . . . I thought he might be onto something. He could hear so well."

"That's exactly how we found him, Whistler — with his ear to the ground. We thought he had caught the hoof beats of a herd."

"A herd — or something else," the Whistler said.

"What else?"

"The Whisperers," the Whistler replied and slid his eyes to one side, almost as if he was afraid to say the words.

"The Whisperers?" the other wolves asked.

"You know the ringing rocks?" the Whistler asked.

"Yes, of course," Mhairie said. "Everyone knows about the ringing rocks. They are scattered all over the Beyond.

But what do they have to do with anything?" Mhairie pressed.

The Whistler paused before answering, as if gathering strength to speak. "In this strange weather, the rocks seem to whisper into the ground. They whisper if you scratch them with your claws. It's a messaging system among certain wolves."

"Certain wolves?" Faolan asked.

"Yes, desperate wolves. They don't want to howl, for then all would know."

"But why? Are they stealing food from their clans?"

"No . . . no, they are summoning Skaarsgard to . . . to . . . take them up." The Whistler almost choked as he spoke.

Dearlea's eyes grew so immense that it seemed as if a green light suffused the dimness of the whelping den. "They are begging for death?"

"Dancing for death," the Whistler rasped.

"What?" The four wolves were so astonished they could hardly utter another word. Edme tossed her head as if attempting to shake off what she'd heard.

"Have you seen it, Whistler?" Faolan asked.

"No, but the rumors fly about faster than owls — and owls, by the way, have seen it. I'm sure," the Whistler replied.

Faolan shut his eyes tight. How he wished he could find Gwynneth. He could not count the moons since he had last seen her.

The Whistler continued. "I haven't seen it myself, but I've heard about it. I met up with Creakle about a moon or so ago. There's a lot of it down in the MacDuff territory. You know how superstitious they have always been."

Edme wrinkled up her face in thought. "Are you sure that it could not have been some way of trying to call the herds? You know, hearken them to their summer feeding grounds?"

"They weren't calling herds, Edme. They were calling Skaars, and that is what they call themselves — Skaars dancers. The dance is spreading and the wolves are dying, dying because they exhaust themselves."

"But how does the messaging system work?" Edme asked.

"They scratch on the rocks to send out a message that calls to the Prophet."

"Prophet?" Faolan asked. "What prophet?"

"They think this prophet is some sort of link on the Great Chain between earth and the ladder of Skaarsgard."

"What?" The four wolves were aghast. This was getting worse and worse.

"You can't tinker with the Great Chain. The Great Chain *is* the Great Chain," Mhairie blurted out fiercely.

Edme spoke with a sharp edge to her voice. "Gnaw wolves know this better than anyone. Our first task when we return to our clan is to start gnawing the Great Chain on bones. On average, a gnaw wolf has gnawed one thousand bones with the Great Chain by the time he gets to the Ring. Let me assure you there are no links to be added or subtracted. To do so would be grounds for immediate expulsion from the Beyond. There is no prophet."

"What you say is true, but it does not mean they are not calling to one. They are," the Whistler said levelly.

"There's very little sense to be made from any of it," Faolan said.

Outside the den, the wind roared and Faolan wondered if on some ice-sheathed ringing rock a desperate wolf was using the last of its energy to scratch a message of death.

"This was a whelping den, wasn't it?" Edme asked to break the ominous silence that had settled upon them all.

"Yes," Dearlea said. She looked at Faolan, Edme, and the Whistler. "I guess none of you really knew about whelping dens, being gnaw wolves."

"*Tummfraws* were our whelping dens," the Whistler said curtly. His strength was definitely returning. "But it must have been nice," he added softly.

The two sisters nodded. Then Dearlea said quietly, "At least we had a mother — a very good mother — but you three never really had one."

"You know" — the Whistler spoke suddenly as if he sensed that the tension needed to be broken — "Tearlach thought that he had seen his mother once."

"How did he know the wolf he saw was his mother?" Dearlea asked.

"Her ears."

"Her ears!" the sisters exclaimed.

"Yes, he said that if he had had ears, he knew they would look just like those."

"Odd, very odd," Mhairie mused.

But it did not strike Faolan as odd at all. He had met his first Milk Giver, Morag, in the last hours of her life, but when he saw her he realized that she had hovered on the edges of his consciousness throughout his entire life. A wisp of fog passed through his mind, stirring his marrow and then dissolving like mist in the noonday sun. Faolan shivered, and he shook his head almost violently.

"What is it, Faolan?" Edme asked.

"Nothing — nothing really," Faolan said lightly. "Just the edge of an old dream that came back to me. Can't quite remember it really." He turned toward the Whistler. "Whistler, have you heard any description of what this prophet looks like?"

"The only thing I have heard is that" — the Whistler hesitated and glanced at Mhairie — "is that he wears a mask."

"A mask!" they all exclaimed.

Faolan gasped. "You mean like the warrior owls wear in battle?"

"I think so. I don't know of any other kind of mask."

"But how would a wolf get an owl's visor?" Edme wondered aloud.

Faolan groaned. "If only I could find Gwynneth."

The wind was abating. Faolan got up to stretch his legs, and walked toward the mouth of the den to peek out. Ice crystals flowed through the darkening sky like sparkling plumes. He was feeling restless and decided to go out to search for more small game. If the Whistler could get his strength back, they could press on toward the border. He knew his decision to bring the Whistler with them was the right one. It seemed especially so when he thought back on what the sisters, Dearlea and Mhairie, had said about the clans breaking up. What were the exact words of Mhairie? *We are all gnaw wolves now*, and that maybe they would have to become a new clan. Perhaps the time had not yet come for a new clan, but the sisters might be right, and for now they would all go together to the border. And if they could find Streak or Creakle, they would take them as well. No sense in leaving any gnaw wolves behind to eat last and to suffer endless abuse as their packs became more desperate in this endless winter of the summer moons.

CHAPTER ELEVEN

A HERO MARK DISTURBED

GWYNNETH HAD NOT BEEN IN THE Beyond for several moons. With the confounding weather, she had been forced to relocate from a lovely vale between the MacDuff and MacNab territories in the Beyond to the old forge of her auntie, where she had learned her craft.

She missed the Sark and Faolan, but most of all she missed hearing the wild untamed music of the wolves' howling, which she had grown accustomed to over the long years she had spent in the Beyond. Of all the owls, Gwynneth knew and understood the ways of the wolves best.

She could have taken over the forge when her auntie died, but she never wanted to. She thought it would feel as if the old Snowy were looking over her shoulders every time she took up the tongs. But this had not happened during the three moons she had passed in her auntie's old forge in the Hoolian empire — not until this evening.

Gwynneth felt the slightest ruffle pass through from her mantle feathers to her plummels, those softest and most delicate feathers that edged her wings. *Great Glaux*, she thought, and immediately flattened all her plumage to grow instantaneously sleeker and taller. This was the fear reaction in owls, known as *wilfing*. Gwynneth had grown as slender as a sapling limb. She stood perfectly still, but the feeling did not go away. The woods were mystical in the time just before twilight. Vapors floated eerily through the tall pines and fir trees, draping the branches like cloth. *Was it . . . ?* She tried to repress the thought.

Was Auntie not at rest? Did the old Rogue smith of the Silverveil have — as the owls said of scrooms who wandered the earth — unfinished business? The vapors that twined around the trees like white ivy had coalesced into a shape — the shape of a Snowy Owl.

Scrooms were given to muffled and mostly incoherent speech. It was often very difficult to understand what they were saying, what messages they were bringing. It became particularly difficult to understand them if one resisted, as Gwynneth was resisting deep within her gizzard. But finally her auntie's words became clear.

"Disturbed!" The word rang out crystalline and sharp. Gwynneth felt a quiver run along her wing feathers. The mist of the Snowy Owl appeared to tremble and glitter under the light of a fullshine moon. Gwynneth had been clutching a pair of tongs over her fire, but now she dropped them. She felt something slip out from her and rise in the darkness to join the bundle of mist that perched on a limb of the fir tree. And yet she had not twitched a feather — not a plummel, not a covert nor a primary. But still she looked down and saw herself standing by the forge. Her body had *wilfed* to a thinness that was alarming, and her long shadow stretched across the pool of orange light that spilled from the flames of the fire.

Disturbed? she said, but her voice was as muffled as the scroom's once had been. Words floated out of her like bubbles. She wondered whether she was speaking or if her thoughts were simply appearing before her.

It is not I who is disturbed, the scroom replied. Gwynneth felt the voice rather than actually heard it. And it felt just the way it did when Auntie used to scold her.

What disturbance, Auntie?

A . . . *a . . . helmet.* A *visor.*

Whose?

Your . . . your . . . The clarity began to dissolve, the words to blur.

Don't go! Don't go! Gwynneth thought.

Then the answer stirred deep in Gwynneth's gizzard. *Da's. Da's helmet?*

A mark was made for him . . . a hero mark.

But hero marks are for wolves —

A hero mark for a warrior owl beloved by wolves!

Questions boiled in Gwynneth's mind, but Auntie was fading away.

A hero mark for an owl? Even for an owl beloved by wolves, it was peculiar! More troubling, however, was the thought that some creature had disturbed her father's helmet and visor. In the world of owls it was unthinkable. Rogue smiths' helmets, visors, and battle claws were always treated with utmost respect, especially the ones they made for their own use and not for barter. How would her father's scroom ever rest if his helmet had been disturbed? How would he ever perch peacefully in Glaumora by the heavenly forge, where the most beautiful objects were wrought with hammers and tongs made of stars, where the sparks from the fires forged new constellations? Gwynneth almost wept when she thought of her da. How could this have happened?

At that moment an icy draft cut through the forest, rattling the limbs of the trees and shattering the last of Auntie's mist as if it had been ice.

"A hero mark disturbed!" Gwynneth's voice rang out in the woods and sounded ridiculous to her. Had she gone *cag mag* and imagined the entire occurrence? Was she waking or dreaming? She blinked. She had slipped back into her plumage, which was as puffy as ever, as if she had never *wilfed*.

And yet a presence seemed to linger, like a shadow in her gizzard. It was as if the mist of her auntie's scroom had saturated the deepest part of her. She lifted one foot and gently raked her talons through her belly feathers.

Gwynneth had not learned of her father's death until long after the war. She knew that he had not died of his wounds on the battlefield but had lingered, and died some time later. There had been rumors of where he had breathed his last, but nothing more. Gwynneth had gone to his forge and set things in order, thinking that perhaps he had made it back there to die. She had even gone to the Sark of the Slough, whose sense of smell was renowned, and asked for her help. But the Sark could not sniff out a trace of Gwyndor and had finally convinced

Gwynneth to give up her quest. Now someone else had found the grave and violated it, perhaps even taken Gwyndor's battle helm and mask. Gwynneth must take up the task again, find her father's helmet, and set his hero mark to rights.

CHAPTER TWELVE

"How Has It Come to This?"

CLOUDS ROILED OVER THE JAGged, ice-sheathed cairns of the Blood Watch. The night turned lavender as the sun sank, and the cairns spiked the sky like fangs gnawing at the dwindling light.

At this distance it was impossible to ascertain if there were guards standing the Watch. The hackles of the five wolves rose as they stopped and looked at the cairns. They were the boundary between justice and lawlessness, between the civilized world and the savage. Between wolves of the Beyond and wolves of the Outermost.

"You can't really tell from here if there are any wolves on the Watch," Edme said.

"And I think those cairns are farther away than they seem. At least a half day's run," Faolan said.

"Let's call that a walk," Edme said with her usual good humor, but Faolan looked at her. Was she more tired than the rest of them? He remembered how fast she had been when she streaked up on that moose calf. Would she be able to muster the energy to move as quickly now?

"Oh, I just hope we can find Mum." Mhairie's voice was like a soft moan.

Edme and the Whistler exchanged glances.

"Well, all we can do is try," the Whistler replied. He was regaining his strength now on a fairly steady diet of rodents. Still, they were all approaching the edge of starvation. Their stomachs were constantly rumbling, and rodents never satisfied them for long.

Under Mhairie and Dearlea's guidance, the wolves had become experts on slicing into an animal's life-pumping artery and consuming its blood. Every time they did this, the Whistler, Faolan, or Edme would thank the sisters, and the sisters would demur, saying, "Oh, it's just Mum. She's the one you should thank. She taught us everything."

Faolan looked at the sisters as they were speaking of their mother one day. Their pelts had lost their luster, and their hip bones were beginning to jut out from their skin. They had both been such beautiful wolves, and now they were shrinking before his eyes. He turned again to look at Edme. She never complained, and he realized that, oddly enough, he no longer heard her stomach rumbling. It was as if her body were consuming itself. And the rodents seemed to be thinning out; it had been at least three days since they had found a mouse nest.

They paused to search for mice runnels, little channels in the snow that indicated a mouse had passed through a drift to get to its nest.

Dearlea pawed at a snowbank. "Mum said that once when she was a little pup, she and her mum got separated from their pack in a sudden spring storm, and they found a nest of snake eggs and ate them. She told us they weren't that bad."

"But the snakes must all be hibernating right now," Edme said.

Faolan began to think of the bears. They had not spotted a single bear in all their days of travel. Had the peculiar behavior of the weather tricked the bears into thinking it was winter? They wouldn't have enough fat on them to sleep the full year through. Were they tucked into caves, falling into some sort of death sleep?

"Mum said the snake eggs tasted a bit sweet. At least I think she said that," Mhairie said almost desperately. It was as if she were trying to hold on to every memory of

Caila, as if these recollections nourished her, fed her almost like food.

"Remember the time that Mum brought down two snow hares almost at once?" Dearlea asked.

"We helped her, Dearlea. She said it was a practice *byrrgis*. Remember, we had to organize the younger pups, and you and I got to be turning guards."

"Oh, yes. How could I have forgotten that?" Dearlea was clearly shocked.

The sisters' talk of their mother increased as game became scarcer. More memories flowed back to them of lessons their mum had organized, stories she had told them, Litha Eves when they had all danced together under the first sliver of the Moon of the Flies. All this they related to the three *malcadhs*, who had never known their first Milk Givers.

But Faolan, Edme, and the Whistler bore the sisters no ill will and only hoped that they would find Caila. Faolan had become increasingly nervous about her as they traveled toward the western border.

Oddly enough, the five wolves had not come upon any of the dance circles the Whistler had described as they traveled west. Mhairie and Dearlea were beginning to wonder if somehow their friend's imagination had gotten the best of him. The travelers took turns breaking track. Mhairie and Dearlea were so accustomed to running together that they were moving side by side through the drifts, slicing a wide path through the snow.

"Mhairie," Dearlea began. "Not that I doubt the Whistler, but do you think these dance circles could have been some kind of fancy of his imagination?"

"I was thinking the same myself. It's hard to tell now with this deep crusted snow, but we haven't seen any circles since we left the Carreg Gaer — not even a stray paw print."

Dearlea was quiet for a bit. Then she said in a slow, thoughtful voice, "I would never accuse anyone of lying, but maybe the Whistler was just confused."

Just as Dearlea was speaking, the sisters came upon a large mound scraped by the wind. The layer of snow left was frozen hard and revealed a circle of crisp paw prints, a circle exactly like the ones the Whistler had described.

"Oh, no!" Mhairie gulped.

"Wh . . . wha — ?" The question died in Dearlea's throat.

And then the wind shifted and a terrible stench rose from the ground.

Faolan, Edme, and the Whistler arrived in a flash. The wind had driven the stench to them, too.

"A dance circle," Dearlea said, looking up.

"But what is that horrid smell?" the Whistler gasped. The sounds gurgled oddly in his throat.

"In my life I have never —" Edme began.

"It's the rancid smell of a rout," Faolan snapped. "They're here."

"What are you talking about?" Mhairie asked. There was a gold fleck in her eyes that seemed to sparkle with wonder and fear. It kindled something in Faolan, some scrap of memory. But he could not linger on that now. This smell meant danger.

"A rout — that's what the outclanners call their packs."

"But why do they smell so awful?" Edme asked.

Faolan's eyes seemed to grow dim. The four wolves waited silently. It was as if he had retreated to another place, another time. "Long ago when I went in search of Thunderheart, I went to the Outermost. I . . . I . . . had an encounter with some outclanners." He took a deep breath. His lungs filled with the noxious air that swirled about them. "The reason they smell like this is because . . . they eat one another."

"What!" the other wolves gasped.

"What are you saying, Faolan?" The Whistler stepped closer. His breath was hoarse, as if it were being torn from his chest.

"I am saying they eat one another and not merely when they are starving. For sport!"

The other wolves were horrified. Their tails dropped and their hackles rose.

"You can't be serious," the Whistler protested. He blinked in disbelief.

"B . . . but . . ." Edme stammered, and her thin body swayed a bit. "They were dancing here. Are you saying when they are dancing they would . . ." She could not bring herself to say the words.

"Possibly," Faolan replied. "Possibly, but I don't see any blood here." He looked down at the footprints.

"Sport, you say?" Mhairie asked weakly. "They eat one another for sport?"

"They have what they call *craws* — it's a fight to the death between two animals."

"Terrible! Terrible." Mhairie and Dearlea kept repeating the word in raw whispers as they backed away. The Whistler followed, but Edme stayed by Faolan's side as he examined the prints.

Finally, they turned to join the other three and then pushed on toward the arching spine of ice. There were more dance circles, each bearing a trace of the outclanners' stench. But the smell didn't bother Faolan as much as the prints he had seen. Edme was loping ahead as point wolf to break track, and although it was not his turn to relieve her, Faolan hurried to join her.

"What are you doing here?" she asked. "It's not your turn yet and this snow is easier. I really don't need your help."

"I didn't come to help. I came to talk."

"Get on my other side so I can see you." Faolan cut behind her. "Something must really be disturbing you if you came up on my blind side."

"It is," Faolan replied.

"The prints, right? At the circle the sisters found?"

"How did you know?" Faolan asked.

"I saw them, too."

"Do you think Caila could have been there?"

Edme sighed. "I saw something that could have been a turning guard's paw. But I don't know the MacDuncan paw prints as well as you do. Did the Whistler say anything?"

"Not a word." Faolan paused. "But the real point is that there were pack wolves dancing, not just outclanners. I think I saw a MacDuff print."

"Did you catch any familiar scent marks at that circle?" Edme asked.

"How could I catch anything in the thickness of that rout stench?"

Edme stopped in her tracks. "Tell me, Faolan, how has it come to this? How can civilized wolves join lawless ones, savages?"

Faolan nodded toward the ridge. "We think those cairns that guard the border are what separate us from them. But hunger is gnawing us now — gnawing away our spirit, our honor. Everything that makes us wolves of the Beyond has . . . has . . ." Faolan stammered. "Has been broken. The decency that makes us so unlike the outclanners is . . . is . . ." He struggled to get out the words. "It's being destroyed. Hunger rules."

CHAPTER THIRTEEN

The Whisper of Rocks

THE MOON OF THE MOSSFLOWERS was nearly upon them. It had been almost half a moon since they had last eaten real meat, and four days since they had found their last rodents.

"I can't believe these are nourishing at all," Mhairie muttered. She nudged the withered bulb with her nose as if searching for the life-pumping artery her mother had taught her to slash. Faolan looked at her as he munched.

"It's an onion, Mhairie, not a rabbit. Just eat it. I spent my first spring moons eating nothing but onion bulbs and roots. Thunderheart taught me how to dig them, and we're lucky to have found these."

"It's an acquired taste, I think," Edme said, trying her best not to gag.

"When I was in the pack that first winter, everyone laughed at me when I ate the rumen. They always leave that to the gnaw wolves, and gnaw wolves hardly ever eat it. But I ate it and was never really hungry," Faolan said.

"Eating another animal's stomach is not exactly appealing," the Whistler said.

"Perhaps not, but a grass eater's stomach, like a caribou or a moose, is filled with lichen and moss. It's nourishing. Look at the size grizzlies grow to. That should be proof enough."

"You're not exactly tiny," Dearlea said.

"You see! I'm living proof. I ate what my second Milk Giver told me to eat. So eat these roots."

The Whistler got up and went to relieve himself by a rock several paces from the foxes' lair where they had made camp for the evening. He was about to raise his leg when he noticed that the ice sheathing the rock had been scratched off recently and there were claw marks on its dark surface. *Could this be a whispering rock?* He tapped the rock with his own claws. Nothing. How hard did one have to tap or claw? He dragged the five toes of his forepaw across the rock's surface. There was a scratchy sound and then beneath it a distinct hiss. He felt a delicate vibration through the ice he was standing on. The ice was a conduit! A perfect channel for the sound. *How strange!* the Whistler thought.

But a few seconds later something even weirder occurred. The rock the Whistler stood near began to hiss — hiss with no provocation — and beneath his feet he once again felt a vibration. Almost like a whisper. The rock and the earth were whispering to him! Someone was sending a message or replying to what he had scratched.

The Whistler tried scratching several more times, and each time there was a response. *This must be what Tearlach heard*, the Whistler thought. But he did not recall a rock near where they had found Tearlach's body. Had Tearlach's hearing been so acute that he could pick up the messages directly from the frozen ground, from the conduit of ice? *Oh, if only I had the listening skills of that dear old earless wolf, I might be able to tell where these whispers are coming from!* thought the Whistler.

But then he had an idea. Deep in the Whistler's crooked throat was a hole through which the drafts and winds of his inhalations and his exhalations streamed. Often he would pick up the edges of maverick winds and gusts when he opened his mouth to howl. A curious alchemy occurred between these winds and his own expirations that transformed his croaking voice into beautiful liquid notes that rose in the darkness of the night and seemed to touch the moon. He could close the hole to make higher notes or open it wider and feel the harmonics quavering in the back of his throat and then blooming into the night in a soulful resonance.

What would happen if he pressed his neck to the ground? He knew exactly where, deep within the channel of his throat. Could he catch the vibrations emanating from the whisper rock? The owls used the stars to navigate and their own hearing to locate the position of prey. A Barn Owl could hear so well that it could detect the heartbeat of a mouse on the ground a hundred feet below. It could contract and expand the muscles of its facial disks to funnel in the sound to its unevenly placed ear slits. The Whistler had a hole in his throat. He could close it and open it. He could very possibly rotate his neck in some way so as to funnel these vibrations to that odd throat of his and perhaps locate the source of a sound.

"Urskadamus! What are you doing? I thought you came here to relieve yourself."

"Shussh!" The Whistler flashed the whites of his eyes.

Faolan fell silent immediately. After several seconds, the Whistler got up, walked a few feet away, and released a hot stream of urine. He then walked back to where he had lain with his throat pressed to the ground. The snow had melted in the spot. He wagged his tail. He looked proud, almost smug — an expression rarely seen on the face of a gnaw wolf.

"My dear fellow," the Whistler began. "You are standing next to a ringing rock — or a whispering rock, as they call them now. And I have just picked up a communication."

"You mean a whisper?"

"Indeed. And I have determined its source."

"How did you ever do that?" Faolan looked with wonder at the Whistler.

"I believe it is essentially the same way owls do it."

Faolan nearly jumped with excitement. "I know all about it from Gwynneth. She's a Masked Owl, which is part of the Barn Owl family. She does this all the time. They tip their ear slit this way and that way and home in on a source."

"Well, now I've done it. Maybe I'm part owl!"

Faolan felt a shiver run through his marrow. He shook his head slightly and the guard hairs on his ruff stood rigid.

"*Lochin* crossed your bones again?" the Whistler asked.

"No, nothing. Nothing at all. But this is really valuable!"

"Do you think we should go have a look?" the Whistler asked.

Faolan hesitated a minute. He had not told the Whistler what he and Edme suspected — that the paw prints in the dance circles they had found were not exclusively outclanner wolves. "Yes, I think we should. But first we have to continue toward the Blood Watch."

The Whistler seemed to hesitate.

"What is it?" Faolan asked.

"The source is coming from close to the Blood Watch."

"What?"

"Not exactly right from it, but it's in the direction we would travel."

"Then we have to be careful because . . . Well, obviously from the circle we have seen so far, these tracks are outclanners — remember. Outclanners who must have slipped through the Blood Watch."

"All of the tracks, Faolan?" the Whistler asked.

Faolan looked into those intelligent green eyes. So the Whistler knew about the clan wolf tracks as well.

CHAPTER FOURTEEN

Rabbit-Ear Moss

SHE SHOULD TAKE IT AS A SIGN, Gwynneth thought, an indication that she was doing the right thing. The sign was a thermal — a draft of warm air that made flying effortless. Without having to stir a feather, she could soar on the billowing air. She shut her eyes and felt herself lift almost magically. Good Glaux, it was great to be a bird! Not just a bird but an owl! She couldn't remember the last time there had been such a draft. The only thermals to be found generally were over the Ring of Sacred Volcanoes. But Gwynneth was nowhere near the Ring now.

The winds were definitely favoring Gwynneth's search for the place where her father had died, the place with a hero mark. Her father, Gwyndor, had always been close to the wolves. He had understood them as no other owl did, and he had passed his passion for the wolves and their traditions on to her. In terms of the sparse company she kept, Gwynneth, like her father, preferred that of wolves to owls. And she realized that if she was going to find her father's helmet and visor, it was a wolf's sniffer that she needed. Not just any sniffer — but the renowned nose of the Sark of the Slough.

The Sark was Gwynneth's closest friend in the Beyond. Gwynneth had often wondered how the old she-wolf was faring since the herds had vanished. It was so much easier for owls. They required less sustenance and the prey that owls sought was small — rodents, and the occasional snake. Small creatures that did not migrate or demand such immense expenditures of energy to hunt as the big ones of the meat trails. One could always depend on finding a vole or two in the burrows beneath nut trees, and there were myriads of such trees, from chestnut to walnut, in Silverveil. So, although Gwynneth usually brought the Sark coals in her coal bucket, this time she had layered wet moss over the coals and then wrapped three voles from her stash in more moss to carry them west toward the Slough and the Sark's encampment.

There was a thick cloud cover over the Slough, but she was pleased when she plunged through it to see a tendril of smoke coming up from the Sark's kiln. *Good*, she thought. *She's not out of fuel yet.*

The Sark caught Gwynneth's scent as she circled high above. The scent of a Masked Owl laced through with the smell of embers, moss, and very savory voles! Her mouth watered in anticipation. For although she generally avoided rodents, starvation was preferable to the thought of one more tern egg. She had discovered that the tern eggs were not really rotten at all, or at least not in the sense of being spoiled. It was simply their natural flavor. The tern's flavor matched its character, which was, in the Sark's opinion, the most annoying of any bird on earth. Flying weasels, she called them. Sharp beaked, skittish, and ridiculously territorial, terns darted down and tried to stab anything that set foot on what they considered their ground. Well, the Sark had taught them a lesson years ago. She had leaped right up and whacked them back. After a few dead terns, the rest left her in peace and avoided the Sark's encampment.

Gwynneth lighted down.

"Well, where in the name of Glaux, to use an owl phrase, have you been?"

"Silverveil, ma'am. It was impossible to tend a forge here."

Owls often addressed the Sark as "ma'am." Gwynneth was not sure when this practice began. Perhaps it was her father, Gwyndor, who started with this form of address, for he had an immense respect for the Sark and had frequently complained of the wolves' treatment of her. Gwyndor abhorred that they often referred to her as a witch. So he had told Gwynneth it was particularly important to call the Sark "ma'am" when any wolves were around. "That'll show 'em the proper respect!" he would often say.

Gwynneth continued, "I didn't feel it right to try to compete for game here with the wolves." She paused. "Not that I bring down caribou or any big meat. But I did bring you some vole. Sorry. I know wolves don't particularly care for rodents."

"Believe me, after tern eggs!"

"Oh, dear, it's come to that?"

"It certainly has — at least for me."

"You look well."

"Don't be ridiculous. I never look well, not even presentable. But those voles smell great."

"I wrapped them in rabbit-ear moss and set them on the coals. I brought you some coals as well."

"That was very kind of you."

"Eat them slowly. They're rich, you know, because they feed on nuts. I wouldn't want to upset your stomach."

"After the insults of the tern eggs, nothing can offend my stomach." The Sark pawed at the moss wrapping and uncovered a vole that was a bit scorched. She sniffed. "It's a haunting aroma, really."

"It's the rabbit-ear moss. It smells that way when it's wet." Heedless of Gwynneth's warning to eat slowly, the Sark devoured the little rodent in a matter of seconds.

"I take it your visit is not entirely a relief effort," she commented with the last bite.

Gwynneth was immediately embarrassed. She should have known it was not simply the Sark's sense of smell that was keen. The Sark's other instincts were honed to a sharpness beyond the ordinary. There was no use evading. The Sark would never let herself be played for a fool.

"You're right, b . . . bu . . . but —"

"Out with it, Gwynneth. I've known you a long time and your father, Gwyndor, even longer."

"It's about Da," Gwynneth blurted out. "I know. I know. You looked for his body when you heard about his death but . . ." the owl said apologetically.

The Sark sighed deeply. "*We*, my dear. Remember I took you out with me. And what did we find?"

"Nothing." Gwynneth cast her eyes down and shifted from one foot to the other nervously.

"So what makes you think we'd find him now?"

"Well, just possibly there's a hero mark someplace for him. A hero mark with his helmet and visor."

"Have you gone *cag mag*? Since when do owls have hero marks?"

"I know . . . I know it sounds crazy."

"So why are you saying this?"

"A scroom . . ." Gwynneth said hesitantly.

"Oh, great Lupus above!" The Sark almost exploded. Her skittish eye went into paroxysms and seemed to bulge out and twirl as if it had a life of its own. And though there was no wind, her pelt seemed to be hosting its own private typhoon. Her fur clattered with the sound of icicles hanging from her withers and chest. "Really, Gwynneth, you know my feelings about scrooms, mist, whatever. It's no more than a bunch of caribou scat! I don't believe in them — *the supernatural*, whoo, whoo!" she intoned in a falsely spooky voice.

"Don't be like that!" Gwynneth's plumage suddenly flattened as she *wilfed* in despair. The Sark was shocked by her reaction.

"Like what?"

"You're mocking me."

"But I don't believe in scrooms."

"It doesn't matter to me what you believe." Gwynneth cocked her head and looked at the Sark with her deep black eyes. "It's what I believe. You should have the decency to hear me out." She paused. "Please, ma'am."

For one of the few times in her life, the Sark felt something akin to remorse. She admired this owl. She admired Gwynneth for smithing art in her forge instead of weapons. Gwynneth had always been a keen student of the ways of wolves and had mastered their language, which, although not entirely different from that of owls, was tricky enough. This, too, was commendable. Gwynneth knew their stories, their histories, and their laws. And perhaps most admirable of all, Gwynneth had befriended the *malcadh* Faolan when he was still a lone wolf. If not for Gwynneth, Faolan might never have found his way to the MacDuncans and ultimately the Watch, where he was quickly proving himself to be a wolf of extraordinary talents. She deserved better than to be mocked.

"All right. I beg your pardon. Tell me about this scroom."

"It was Auntie," Gwynneth replied softly and began

her story of how the vaporous mist had hung in the trees and told her of an unsettled spirit — of her father, Gwyndor.

"Now forget the hero mark part, but what's this about a helmet and visor?"

"Wherever my da's helm and visor were . . . were when he died, they have been moved." She paused and spoke the single word clearly and with emphasis: "Disturbed." She knew that the Sark would understand the significance of this single word in connection with a forged article, particularly a helmet and visor made by a Rogue smith.

The Sark grew very still and shut her eyes tightly. The helm and visor of an owl — a Guardian Owl — on the head and body of a wolf. She had noted the details of that mask and helm, but would there be enough in the jugs to stir up an older memory?

"Come with me," the Sark ordered and began walking toward her cave.

Gwynneth followed. The fire that the Sark usually kept, by which many a she-wolf had rested after being driven from a clan for birthing a *malcadh*, had dwindled. They walked past it. The Sark was leading Gwynneth to the darker recesses of the cave. On the walls, jugs and pots of all shapes and sizes rested on ledges or were suspended on cords of caribou sinew. "Wait here," the Sark said suddenly.

It was pitch-black, but absolute darkness never bothered an owl. Gwynneth could see as clearly as if it were broad daylight. The Sark must have realized this, for she deliberately turned her back to block Gwynneth's view. Gwynneth heard a slight clink as the Sark set a clay jug on the floor and then what sounded like a deep inhalation, as if the Sark were taking a huge breath. But the Masked Owl did not smell anything, and that is where she and the Sark parted ways.

For as she pressed her muzzle into the long neck of the jug, the Sark had entered a landscape of scents. Fired in her own kiln, glazed with the slips and clays from the streambeds of the Beyond, the Sark's memory jugs were filled with impressions, memories, and descriptions of scents. Memory was sacred to the Sark, a hallowed power of the brain fed by tributaries of scent. And now she felt as if she were caught in a mad river of crosscurrents and eddies, rapids, whirlpools, and surges.

She pulled down another jug, then another. Gwynneth could hear the deep inhalations growing more shallow. The owl could even hear the acceleration of the Sark's heartbeat.

Through the scented landscapes flashed a light — *The glint, the glint! The metallic shimmer. But the smell . . . that lovely smell. How often Gwyndor perched near my kiln with the fragance of rabbit-ear moss still in his head feathers. The light of the flames from my kiln on that helm — but it was all so different from when the wolf that jiggered about. That fool dancing wolf.*

"Ma'am! Ma'am!" Gwynneth was hovering just over the Sark's face, fanning her with her broad wings. "Are you all right!"

"Rabbit-ear moss!" The Sark's eyes flew open.

"Are you all right? You fainted or something."

"It's the 'or something,' my dear!" The Sark staggered to her feet and seemed none the worse for wear. She gaped at the array of jugs.

"You kept shouting about rabbit-ear moss."

"Yes, of course. That was the trigger, don't you see?"

Gwynneth shook her head in bewilderment.

"You brought the voles in that rabbit-ear moss. It was scorched, so I didn't quite recognize it, but then — why, yes, the flanges!"

"Flanges? What in the world are you talking about?"

"The glint came off the visor, and I recollected it in my memory jug. The flanges! I was such a fool. How could I have missed it?"

"Missed what, ma'am?"

"You know the special trim that your father, Gwyndor, made where the visor slid down from the helmet — it was a rather signature design of his. But it was so long since I've seen it, and I hate to make excuses, but I was absolutely nauseous from some tern eggs. . . . I didn't recognize the helmet as Gwyndor's!"

"Yes, he did make lovely flanges — they were like a flat rim and allowed the visor to slide up and down on the helmet with a flick of the head. But I still don't understand."

"Don't owls often pack their helmets with rabbit-ear moss for cushioning?"

"Yes, it's quite a common practice."

"But not with this wolf — he didn't know, nor did he need the cushioning. Fur's as good as moss, most likely."

"What are you talking about?"

"I saw your father's helm, Gwynneth! But not on an owl — on a wolf!"

"What?" Now it was Gwynneth who staggered and felt faint.

CHAPTER FIFTEEN

Dance Interrupted

THE SNOWBANKS AND DRIVING winds slowed the journey toward the cairns. Though they had appeared so close, it took a day and most of a night to reach them. The five wolves had drawn up just beneath the looming blue shadow of the icy battlements of the Blood Watch, near the source of the whispers they were tracking. Very few of the cairns were topped.

"Great Lupus!" Edme murmured, squinting toward the ridge. "How do they keep watch? There are at least thirty cairns, and only four or five wolves up there."

"Maybe at this distance and in this light, we can't see them all. When we get closer, there might be more wolves," the Whistler offered.

"Let's hope," Faolan said, although there was not a trace of hope in his voice.

"I wonder if the Prophet will be there?" Dearlea asked.

"I don't know. We've seen so many circles between the Shadow Forest and here that it's hard to imagine he could be in so many places at once," Faolan said. "And I would hope if he were, the Blood Watch would stop him — her — whatever. Stop the dancing."

"I think it spreads," Edme said. "It's like a disease, this dance. Maybe this prophet started it, but he can't be there for everybody." She paused. "Not like Skaarsgard." She looked up at the sky. It was too cloudy to see any constellations. "I bet you anything this so-called prophet is just an ordinary wolf."

"An ordinary, starving wolf," Mhairie added, "whose brain has become addled from starvation and his marrow thinned. He might not even be a bad wolf. Just a stupid wolf with some idiot idea."

Edme lifted her muzzle into the breeze. "The wind is coming our way. I think we've found a dance circle!"

"I am already picking up the stench of the outclanners." Mhairie wrinkled her nose.

"Yes, the wind favors us, so they might not pick up our scent. And that fox den gave us a good cover scent if the wind should shift. Let's see what we have. But we're just going to watch, and not *engage*." Faolan said the last word with emphasis.

They made their way as close as they could to the source of the whispers. As they crested a small rise, they spotted a broad circle with several wolves dancing.

"Look!" Edme said.

"Are they really moving? It seems so slow," Dearlea whispered.

"One is falling down," Faolan said.

They had no idea how long the wolves had been dancing, but they seemed to be in a deep trance. They moved unthinkingly through the steps as if almost asleep. It was the oddest thing any of the five travelers had ever seen. The dancing wolves were twirling slowly, their steps somehow freakish. In the wasting light of the moon, under a sky reeling with stars, these creatures looked as if they had lost their essence, their defining marrow. They had the bodies of wolves, but inside, it was as if a different animal inhabited their pelts. Their movements were palsied, involuntary jerks and twitches. While dancing they emitted strange wheezes and gurgles so dissimilar to a wolf's normal vocal range that they were incomprehensible.

Edme wondered aloud, "Lord Adair and Lord Jarne were bad, but would they go this far?"

"Hush, let's listen," Faolan ordered. "They've left off those other sounds they were making. They're starting to howl."

The howling began with a warbling ululation similar to the *glaffling* or mourning cry of grieving wolves. At first the words were incoherent, but soon the travelers could make them out.

Kill . . . kill . . . kill the body. Release the soul
We are waiting souls wrapped in our sacred pelts
Skaarsgard, your apostles await you
Gather us to your star fur
Let our marrow join yours
Bring the Cave of Souls to earth
Where we will live again
Death is our life
Dying our meat
Our spirits will feast.

The morbid howling festered in the night air, and yet there was something seductive in the sound. Despite the deep weirdness of the dancers, the five wolves felt a sudden vulnerability stir within their marrow. They knew they must stand strong together. Faolan put a paw on Mhairie's shoulder, and Edme raised her paw and placed it on Dearlea's withers, while the Whistler nuzzled his head protectively on top of Edme's. There was something insidious in the darkness. Insidious and yet enthralling.

So easy, so easy, Faolan was thinking. *So easy to give in. Will I fall in love with death when it finally comes? Does a starving wolf fall in love with famine?*

Some of the dancers, nearing the cusp of exhaustion, collapsed on the ground unconscious.

Dearlea blinked as a caribou pelt fell off of one of the wolves in the dance circle.

"Mum!" she yelped. "It's Mum!"

And it was Caila — Caila, the once proud turning guard of the MacDuncan clan. She stood still as the remaining wolves continued to dance around her. Her eyes were clouded and reflected nothing in the darkness of the night. But there was no stopping Dearlea and Mhairie. They raced down the embankment toward their mother. To Faolan, Edme, and the Whistler, the she-wolf they had known as Caila was barely recognizable. Her unfocused eyes seemed to spin in her head as madly as the Sark's. Her once lustrous blond pelt had turned dull and brownish. In many places there were bald patches with old blood and dark yellows and browns that came from tree bark smeared on her bare skin. As the moon rolled out from behind the clouds, the shadows of the dancing wolves leaped around her, and it seemed as if she were ensnared in a macabre web.

"Mother!" Mhairie skidded to a stop in front of Caila. "It's us. Your pups. Me — Mhairie — and Dearlea."

"Oh, Mum!" Dearlea cried.

Caila blinked and for just a second the sisters caught a glimpse of a familiar bright glint in her eyes. There was a glimmer of tenderness, and then the eyes turned dark and the light died.

Caila peeled back her lips and growled. It was a strange gesture, half threat and half fear. Her ears did not fold back but twitched as if caught in a spasm. "I am not your mum. I have never been your mum. Never! Never!"

"No, Mum!" Mhairie cried and shook her head. "We're your daughters!" Mhairie pleaded while Dearlea simply looked on, stunned beyond words.

"No! No! I was your wet nurse. No more." Caila staggered slightly and her eyes came into focus. "You two were the right ones in the litter of three. The third was a *mal-*

cadh. And you know the laws." She had lapsed into a singsong voice. Her tone was almost silly but had an edge of mockery. "Your true Milk Giver was driven from the clan and you two were left with me."

"You can't say that!" Mhairie cried.

"She's mad!" Dearlea gasped.

"I can and I do say it. Eiric was never your father. I was never your mother. I deny you! I deny you! I deny you!"

To deny three times was the curse of the faithful mate to an unfaithful partner. But it was never uttered to children. Never!

CHAPTER SIXTEEN

The Cave Before Time

"WE'RE YOUR DAUGHTERS," DEARLEA pleaded for the third time. And just as Caila was about to respond, an outclanner came out of nowhere and lunged for a wolf that had collapsed on the ground in a stupor. The outclanner misjudged his leap and landed on Caila. There was a terrible shriek as his fangs sunk into her flanks. Faolan and Edme both leaped on the attacking wolf and rolled him, but he was quick and strong for such a thin creature, and he reeked of dead wolf. Within seconds Faolan realized that the outclanner stalked the dancing circles and devoured the wolves who had dropped from exhaustion. He was a wolf eater.

Faolan had never experienced outrage as strong as what coursed through him. It felt as if his marrow were on fire. The wolf eater wheeled about to confront him, and Edme watched, transfixed, as Faolan reared on his hind legs. He tossed his head at an odd angle. His green eyes darkened to black and the tips of his guard hairs turned bright white. Suddenly, it seemed to Edme that Faolan had ceased being a wolf. It was as if he had slipped his pelt to become something else, another animal, immense and frightening. He growled. It was not a wolf's growl at all but came from deeper in his chest with a rough, raw resonance that shook the air. Faolan struck out at the wolf with both his paws. The splayed one looked immense and the sound of it connecting with the wolf eater sent a crack around the circle. A second later the wolf's head lopped sideways and dangled ridiculously, and then he collapsed on the ground. It was over.

The four wolves stood in stunned silence. But the other wolves were oblivious and kept dancing, except for Caila, who turned in a daze and began walking away. Snow had begun to fall, and within seconds she dissolved into the whiteness of the night.

Edme turned to the Whistler. "Did you see him?"

"You mean what Faolan did to the wolf — breaking his neck?"

"But . . . but was it really Faolan?"

"What are you talking about?" the Whistler asked.

He didn't see it! Edme couldn't believe it. Surely the Whistler must have seen Faolan's transformation, heard the growl, seen the white guard hairs, or even the peculiar way in which Faolan's narrow muzzle had suddenly broadened, so his nose squashed upward and his nostrils flared. It was the face and the pelt of a grizzly. And did Faolan tear with his fangs as a wolf should? No, he had merely smacked the wolf eater with a mighty blow and instantly snapped his neck. Was she, Edme, the only one who had seen all this?

The outclanner lay dead in the snow, which was now coming down so hard that his body was quickly being covered. The dancing of the other wolves slowed in the thickly falling flakes. The wind suddenly strengthened and slammed into them. The world was turning an impenetrable white.

"We have to get Mhairie and Dearlea out of here," Faolan said. "Look at them." The two sisters were clinging to each other and trembling as they stared into the whiteness that had swallowed their mother.

"We can't leave her!" Dearlea cried. "She's hurt, bleeding."

"We can follow her blood trail," Mhairie said.

"No! Not against this wind. The snow is getting

worse, it's going to be a blizzard," Edme barked. "We have to find shelter. We'll be smothered by it if we don't find a cave, a den. Anything!"

"What about them?" Mhairie said, looking at the Skaars wolves. Only three were dancing now. The rest had collapsed and were quickly becoming mounds in the snow.

"They'll be dead by morning." Faolan's voice was flat. "And so will we if we don't find shelter."

The night had become a featureless world of swirling white. So it was not what Faolan saw but what he heard that alerted him. He shoved his ears forward. The sound of the wind was screeching around them, high and whistling, but beneath the whistle was another sound, a lower warble as if the contours of the landscape around them had shifted. A yawn in the wind made Faolan shut his eyes. Could it be? Could they be that near? Was that gasp in the wind truly . . . "Follow me!" he ordered.

The rhythmic breathing of five exhausted wolves echoed off the walls of the cave to wrap around Edme. *It's a cocoon of dreams*, she thought. She fervently wished that the sleep of Mhairie and Dearlea was dreamless — void of any memories of their mother. The Whistler — did he dream? In the brief time he had been with them he had regained his strength, though he was still stick thin.

And Faolan, what were his dreams? Edme wondered. She looked over at her sleeping friend. His muzzle was long and narrow, like that of a wolf. His nostrils were no longer flared, and the tips of his guard hairs were the same color as the rest of his fur — silver, not white. She remembered how half a moon or more back, he had come into their den on the scouting expedition, shimmering with frost, huge, but so fragile, like a creature from another time. Like a frost wolf. "Another time," she whispered to herself and looked around the cave.

This cave was a strange place and also felt as if it existed in another time. *Almost another world*, thought Edme. How had Faolan found it? The light inside was dim, but she opened her single eye wide and felt something else open inside her. There was a sudden illumination, as if a piece of moonlight had fallen into the cave. She looked about, and in the flickering silvery light, she saw the forms of all manner of animals leaping, running, and flying. There seemed to be a *byrrgis* of wolves streaking across the rock surface of the cave. The flat lines drawn on the rock wall suggested motion and hinted at a story — a very old story.

For Faolan sleeping beside her, those drawings pulsed with life. While Edme heard the rhythmic breathing of her sleeping companions, Faolan heard the breath of the scores of animals running across the rock face. He heard the pounding of caribou hooves, the nearly silent stirrings of the owls' wings as they flew above the *byrrgis*. In his sleep, he heard and felt them all.

As Faolan slept, he felt something flow out of his marrow to another self. *This is not a dream*, he thought. *This is real.* A very real part of himself exited his sleeping body and hovered above him for a few brief seconds. It drifted almost lazily through a maze of passageways in the cave. *Ah, yes*, he thought, as he encountered a blank wall with no drawings. He picked up a fragment of black rock in his mouth and began to scratch on the wall. *A new picture. Time for a new picture.* The thought did not seem odd to him in the least. Had he done this before in the gyre of time?

His paw felt unusually nimble, but he did not question anything. He simply knew that it was crucial that he record the terrible sight of the Skaars dancers and the savage outclanner who had come to feed on the unconscious wolves. Faolan had killed him with one swift blow to the head. But it was not the wolf spirit within him that killed the outclanner. It was the spirit of another animal, a bear. Faolan looked down to see he was not holding the rock fragment in his teeth, but in his paw. But his paw had changed; it was now the same paw that had delivered that fatal blow — a bear's paw. *How interesting*, he observed in a detached manner.

And then he was once more hovering over his sleeping body. What had been divided began to come together again, a knitting of marrows as one spirit flowed back into another. The sleeping body stirred ever so slightly. Just before Faolan drifted back into consciousness, Caila's words streamed through his mind. *You two were the right ones in the litter of three. The third was a* malcadh. *And you know the laws.*

And I was the third, Faolan thought. *I was the* malcadh. In the year of his birth, only one *malcadh* had been born into the MacDuncan clan. And it had been he. Mhairie and Dearlea were his sisters.

Faolan woke with a start and rose to his feet. He knew two things now — one truth from his dream journey through the cave, and one that he had felt ever since he had noticed the golden flecks in Mhairie's and Dearlea's eyes. He had seen that shimmering gold before — behind the milky film in the eyes of Morag, his first Milk Giver.

The young she-wolves were waking now. Faolan walked over to them.

"What is it, Faolan?" Dearlea asked. He tipped his head to one side and peered deeply into their eyes.

"You had a mother before Caila. Our mother — Morag. I am the *malcadh* who was cast out, and you were the two pups who were saved. Dearlea, Mhairie, you are my sisters. She would have loved you dearly — your first Milk Giver."

"What?" the sisters gasped.

"Faolan, you mean she was driven from the clan because of you? And we — Mhairie and I — were given to Caila — a second Milk Giver?"

"Yes. That is the law for the sisters of a *malcadh*," Faolan replied. "And Caila loved you. She did. You must believe that."

The sisters' eyes swam with confusion.

"She was sick when she denied you. She is sick. Can't you see it?"

They both stared at him silently. He could not read their expressions. Did it mean nothing to them that they now had a brother? Or were they perhaps ashamed? Did they blame him for their real mother being driven from the clan?

And I have another secret, Faolan thought. *Before I was born a wolf, I had a thunderous heart in my chest. The heart of a grizzly bear.* But this truth, Faolan would tell no one.

CHAPTER SEVENTEEN

A Sudden Summer

"WELL, TOO BAD THE BLIZZARD slammed down on us. But it has eased now. So we might as well start here." The Sark plunged into a mountainous drift.

"You can't be serious, ma'am!" Gwynneth found herself addressing the scrawny butt of the Sark, who seemed to have been swallowed almost whole by the snowdrift.

The Sark surfaced a few seconds later in a soft explosion of powdery white.

"You were saying?" she asked.

"I was saying you can't seriously be trying to find scent traces in all this!"

"One has to begin someplace," the Sark replied tersely.

"Can you smell anything?"

"There are traces down there, but it's difficult. I'm going to do a little digging now that I've at least made something of a dent. So far, the spoor is pointing us north and west."

"Toward the Outermost?" Gwynneth's voice quavered, but the Sark was so absorbed in her task of digging out the drift that she didn't notice. Gwynneth couldn't help but admire her tenacity.

"Oh, if there were only a Burrowing Owl around! They can dig with those long legs of theirs. I'm sorry I can't be of more help, ma'am."

"Don't worry about it. Your talents will be used."

It was not the first time the Sark and the Masked Owl had worked together. As the Sark often reminded Gwynneth, the two of them together were more than the sum of their parts. As the Sark put it, "With my sniffer and your ear slits, we've got it all."

The Sark might not believe in scrooms, but she did believe in honor and duty. And it was Gwynneth's duty to find her father's helmet and visor and to try to restore his hero mark as best she could. Gwynneth could not be absolutely certain where this grave was, but if she could find his helmet, she knew in her gizzard that she would somehow be guided there. *I know it! I just know it!* But she was startled at the idea that her father's bones might rest in the Outermost.

The Sark had surfaced once again. She looked perplexed, or rather as perplexed as a creature could look with mismatched eyes, one of which was spinning crazily.

"Well?" Gwynneth said anxiously.

"It's odd, but I do believe that somehow the effects of starvation are altering —"

"Oh, no!" Gwynneth gasped. "Your sniffer is off?"

"What? Are you *yoicks*? Of course my sniffer isn't off!"

Gwynneth knew instantly that she had said the wrong thing. One never doubted the Sark — at least not out loud.

"It's the scents that have changed," the Sark huffed. "A wolf doesn't smell quite the same when it's starving. It alters something in them. I'm getting a little whiff of MacDuff, possibly MacAngus — I'm not sure, though — and maybe some old musk ox. Musk ox used to circle up around here." She paused dramatically and managed to still her eye. "And, there's something else!"

"What?" Gwynneth asked. She felt a small stitch in her gizzard. *Do I really want to hear this?*

The Sark walked up to the Masked Owl and lifted a snowy paw to pat her shoulder. "Owl bones."

"Da?"

"I don't know, dear. A dead owl smells different from a living owl. I only knew your father when he was very much alive, 'in full gizzard' as he would often say when he had accomplished something masterful at his forge. I smelled traces from his forge when I first saw the wolf in that mask. I just didn't realize it until I consulted my memory jugs. It makes sense, don't you see?"

The Masked Owl blinked.

"Gwynneth, the wolf was wearing a helmet and visor made in your father's forge. The helmet still carried traces of scent with it. Your father used an odd mixture of bonk embers and lower-grade coals. He also used some caribou scat."

"You mean poop."

"Yes, you owls call it 'poop.' So undignified! I call it 'scat.' No matter. It's an unusual combination of fuels for fires. But who am I to judge? Each artist has his own formulas for heat."

"So the wolf who wore the helmet carried scents left over from the forge of my father."

"One might deduce."

Gwynneth only vaguely knew the meaning of the word "deduce." She sensed that the Sark did not want to say for sure what animal had disturbed the hero mark. For all her confidence, the Sark often hedged her bets and exercised a certain amount of caution.

"What we have now," the Sark continued, "is reliable spoor. More reliable, I might add, than the scent of a starving wolf. I think wolf scents in this time of famine are becoming mutable. There is an underlying acrid scent to a starving wolf that dilutes its base scent. It makes it quite confusing. But I can follow a scent trail of owl bones and forge smells. We can begin."

But how? Gwynneth wondered. *How can the Sark have the energy to track?* The Sark had hardly eaten anything save for the voles and some Slough tern eggs. Gwynneth knew that the Sark did not especially like rodents or any of the small creatures that comprised the owl's basic diet. But she would have to learn to stomach them if they were going to track a scent trail through heavy snow.

And she did.

"I can't say that I find snake exactly delicious — that would be an overstatement — but I think I prefer it to rat," the Sark said.

It was their third day out, and the spoor trail was patchy at best. It went this way and it went that way. But the Sark was showing strength and energy and her usual persistence. When they holed up in an abandoned den or cave for rest, they often passed the hours in lengthy discussions about everything from the best fuels for fires to food.

"What about the snake eggs I found this morning?" Gwynneth asked.

"Definitely superior to Slough tern eggs. That of course is damning with faint praise. I can't help but think my distaste for Slough tern has something to do with their obnoxious personalities. Although I suppose that's something of a paradox — perhaps I should enjoy eating a creature that I find offensive in life."

"I can't believe you just said that, ma'am," Gwynneth replied.

"Why ever not?" the Sark asked.

"You admire the caribou, don't you? You consider them a noble breed."

The Sark did not answer immediately. Her eye gave a skittish turn in its socket. "Ah! I see where this is going. Yes, I admire the caribou, I think they are noble. And so delicious! Point taken, Gwynneth. You are a clever owl."

They were well into the Moon of the Mossflowers, perhaps one of the most beautiful of the summer moons. It was during this time that the harsh ground of the Beyond burst into flower with delicate white blossoms springing from the mossy expanse of the land. The blooms were no bigger than the dew claw of a pup and added a shimmer to the Beyond. Some wolves referred to this as the Moon of the Two Skies, for when darkness fell, it seemed as if both earth and sky were abloom with stars. This came in the middle of the summer moons and was normally the hottest time of the year. Soon after, the cooler ones blew through, beginning with the Caribou Moon. On its heels, like a point guard on prey in a *byrrgis*, came the Moon of the Frost Stars, the mildest of the three hunger moons. But this year, each moon brought only cold and want.

Nevertheless, this particular day dawned with a sudden heat, such as that of an early summer morning. The Sark stepped out of the cave, tipped her head up toward the ferocious sun, and bellowed, "Great Lupus! Enjoy it while it lasts — summer!" The Sark was not fool enough to think that a true summer had arrived, but the ever hopeful Gwynneth spread her wings and rose into the dazzling shafts of sunlight. She whooped joyously. "Glaux almighty, do you think we'll see mossflowers?"

"Don't be ridiculous!" the Sark shouted back. "Is it hot enough to melt all this?" She tossed her head toward the mountainous drifts of snow the blizzard had left behind. "Never. Let's hope for a bit of mushiness."

But she knew that was a fragile hope at best. She wanted to believe the warmth would last, but her nose told her it wouldn't. She could smell the snow winds brewing. No other creature could pick up the elusive scent, but the Sark could open her mouth and almost taste snow in the dry, brittle air. She inhaled deeply to feel the warmth of the air, but on the back side it carried a coldness that flooded her nose. And then the scent went dead. It was hard to smell when all you felt was fear and sorrow. The world she and Gwynneth both loved was dying. Something salty flooded the Sark's throat and nostrils, and she was shocked to realize it was her own tears. *I can't let Gwynneth see me cry! I won't cry!*

She could already feel the ice forming in her marrow and the sunshine only taunted her.

The Sark was right. The warmth only lasted long enough for the immense drifts of snow and ice to grow slushy. But with the softening came sharp new scents, including the scent of meat.

"This is a cache!" the Sark said, sniffing over chunks of caribou and marmot as Gwynneth hovered over her. "Can we eat it? What are the rules about caching?" the Sark asked.

Gwynneth blinked. "I should know?"

"Well, you hang around the Ring of Sacred Volcanoes more than I do. That's where they make the rules, amend the *gaddernock*, and all that business." She spoke with mild contempt.

"But you're the wolf. I'm not," Gwynneth said.

The Sark sighed. She rolled her eyes, and the bushy white tufts of fur that spouted above them sprang to life like two snow hares hopping up and down. "Honestly, Gwynneth. You know how I feel about so much of that wolf nonsense — the elaborate customs, the traditions — all those jangly bone necklaces they wear to symbolize the Great Chain. What a bunch of *racdrops*, as you owls would say. And I wouldn't give a pinch of caribou scat for any of it. So you can hardly consider me a wolf. I've lived alone my entire life. What do I know?"

"Well, ma'am, I can tell you that the wolves of the Watch permit caching food within their own territory. And if a wolf comes across a cache, they can eat it."

"Now, that's helpful," the Sark said encouragingly. "If the Watch wolves have that rule, then I would suppose other clans would as well. What's good for the goose is good for the gander, as they say."

"What do they say!?" Gwynneth had never heard any creature say this. Not even geese who often flew over the Beyond.

"Oh, it's just an old expression."

Gwynneth had certainly never heard it, but she did not question the Sark. For the old wolf shared what she wanted to share and nothing more. The Sark was essentially a deep mystery — her origins, her history, her entire life. She was a country unknown.

The Sark had begun wriggling into the rather small hole where the meat had been cached. She was picking up all sorts of telltale scents from which she could deduce how long the animals had been dead and what they had eaten before they died. There were thus far no indications of the predator who had brought down the prey.

"It's opening up a bit in the rear," she shouted back to Gwynneth. And at that moment, an unexpected scent flooded her nostrils. Her skittish eye spun as it was wont to do on such occasions, and she slapped a paw over it so she could concentrate. Then, inhaling deeply, she began to sort out the odors that had infiltrated her nostrils.

"What'd you find? Anything? Anything at all?" Gwynneth kept up a steady stream of questions, which the Sark ignored while she concentrated on untangling the skein of smells. Then she backed out of the hole and turned around to face Gwynneth, who was hopping up and down, first on one foot, then the other.

"Well? The spoor?"

The Sark took a deep breath and finally spoke. "No, not the spoor. This is rather shocking, Gwynneth. There is a trace of ash and something slightly sulfurous. A wolf of the Watch has been caching here, and not only that —" The Sark's voice jerked. "I can't believe it!"

"Believe what?"

"There's a bone here — a gnawed bone with . . . with . . ." she stammered.

"With what?" Gwynneth was nearly jumping out of her feathers.

"An incised design."

"Of what?" Gwynneth screeched.

"A helmet and visor!"

CHAPTER EIGHTEEN

The Broken Chain

THE FIVE WOLF COMPANIONS HAD emerged from their cave on the day following the blizzard, and reported to the Blood Watch. They had begun serving almost immediately. The Watch was primarily focused on preventing outclanners from slipping over the border, but had also now organized shifts to ambush the scavenger wolves who tried to pick off the fallen Skaars dancers.

"Edme, do you realize that none of the Blood Watch wolves have ever tried to break up a Skaars circle? Don't you think that's odd?" Faolan asked.

"Not exactly. They're stretched. They can barely keep up with running off the scavenger wolves, not to mention chasing the outclanners back across the border," Edme said.

"Yes, but that's not everything, is it?" Faolan looked at her with narrowed eyes. He saw her withers bristle slightly.

He's so perceptive, Edme thought. *There's no sense trying to evade the question.* "Well, you can see an outclanner. You can smell a scavenger — they reek from their very marrow. But this . . . this dancing, this prophet — it's another kind of evil, isn't it?"

A shiver passed through Faolan. "You're right. But even so, don't you think we should try to stop it?"

"Yes," Edme replied. "I'm not sure how, but we should try. I have no doubt the Whistler would join us, but what about Dearlea and Mhairie?"

"They have more reason than any of us. The Skaars dancers stole Caila."

Faolan was right. No one was more eager than his sisters. Soon the five friends had a plan, which they reviewed half a dozen times. The main part of the plan was food. They were bringing the Skaars dancers two snow hares. Tamsen, the captain of the Blood Watch, had given permission for this, although it was clear she didn't have much faith in their endeavor.

"So, first we present them with the food, and as they eat we talk some sense into them," Edme explained again.

"I think," Mhairie said, "you need to explain that you are from the Watch — the Watch of the Sacred Ring, not just the Blood Watch."

"Definitely," the Whistler said. "Direct orders of the Fengo. You have to muster all the authority you can."

"Good point," Faolan said. "We remind them of the Great Chain — how Skaars dancing is a perversion of all they have learned. Whistler, you can howl the song of the Great Chain." He then turned to Dearlea. "Dearlea, you know it, too, don't you?"

"Oh, yes, I was training under Alastrine."

"Good. Begin to howl it as soon as we present the food."

And so they tried. The wind had stilled and the moon was steeped in thick clouds when they left to stalk a circle. They decided to seek out a small circle with no more than five or six wolves and one where the wolves did not appear too exhausted.

When they finally found what they felt to be the perfect test circle, they were able to slip through the shadows and come quite close. When Faolan gave the signal, all five wolves advanced in their most submissive postures.

Faolan and Edme stepped forward and dropped the snow hares. "We are Wolves from the Watch at the Sacred Ring, and we bring you food."

One wolf, a large gray, stopped and stared vacantly at them. The dancing slowed as the others seemed to finally catch the scent. They sniffed the meat, but seemed suspicious.

"Eat!" Edme urged, as the Whistler and Dearlea began howling the song of the Great Chain.

Come listen, ye wolves, we are all part of one
From earth to sky from fire to sun.

One dancer nibbled a bit but then stopped as another wolf stepped forward.

"Go on!" Edme urged. But the dancers would only take the smallest bite before immediately starting to dance again.

"No . . . no, you must eat, not dance!"

"Skaars!" a wolf gasped.

"Skaarsgard is in the heaven," Faolan said. "In the sky, not on earth."

"You drive him off with this meat. I shall not have blood on my muzzle when he descends for me!"

"No blood! No blood! Skaarsgard will not come down!" The cry went up from the dancing wolves and they twirled even faster. The very notion of Skaarsgard descending to earth was so revolting that Faolan's and Edme's ruffs rose stiffly.

"Skaarsgard does not descend," Faolan insisted. "He will call you. You do not call him."

Faolan head-butted a wolf who had been crying, "No blood!"

"Eat! Eat! We bring you good food," Faolan insisted.

But the wolf looked at him dumbly. "You mislead us! The Prophet shall find us violated with blood. Skaarsgard will not touch us."

"His brain is addled!" Faolan whispered.

Edme planted herself in front of the wolf's wagging head. "Listen to me, wolf. Listen to the Song of the Great Chain. You remember the Great Chain, don't you?"

"The Great Chain!" the wolf cried. He tried to leap up as if to catch a link and bring it right down to earth, but his paws had hardly left the ground when his body convulsed. He collapsed, his eyes rolling back into his head. He let out a strangled cry, then all was quiet.

"He's dead," Edme whispered. Dearlea and the Whistler stopped howling.

A dancer nearby stepped delicately over the dead wolf and began to move in a slow stumbling prance away . . . away. Others followed him, away from the meat of the two snow hares and into the moon-streaked night.

CHAPTER NINETEEN

THE OBEA TREE

THE SARK AND GWYNNETH WERE pressing on — the Masked Owl flying overhead as the wolf below traveled in an erratic yet vaguely northwesterly direction to follow the spoor track.

They were just to the south of MacDonegal territory and had found ample signs left by the Skaars dancers. Although it had turned cold once again after that one sunny day, there had not been any more blizzards. The distinctive circles left by dancing paws were clearly visible. Many of the circles bore the unique scent of dream marks, which the Sark found very disturbing. But she did not bother to explain the significance of this to Gwynneth. Some of these dream marks bore the odor of the spoor they were tracking. Others did not. This led the Sark to believe that not all the dancers were led by the wolf in the helmet and visor. Most disturbing of all, however, was that many of the circles had the scent of a wolf about to die. This was a dance that would lead wolves to their ends.

They were drawing near the Outermost now. In the distance, the Sark and Gwynneth could see on the horizon the faint scrawl of the ice cliffs that separated the Beyond from the Outermost. The wind had just shifted and was spilling down over the jagged ridge. The breeze was tinged with a rancid odor that assaulted the Sark's nose and set her eye spinning. Buried in the snow was not a dead wolf but the scat of a live wolf who had devoured its own kind!

The sky that had briefly arched like a limitless blue dome now turned woolly with thick clouds that pressed down upon the Beyond. The clouds seemed almost to have weight, crushing down like a vise upon them, as if to obliterate any hope of escape from the destiny that awaited them. Along the way, they had encountered a few wolves, but they were alarmed to learn that they were often the last remnants of their packs. They had encountered one wolf from the MacAngus clan who informed them that the chieftain had died.

"The chieftain is dead?" The Sark was aghast at this news.

"Yes," Aldwyn MacAngus replied. "The Stone Pack is finished, and I heard tell that the River Pack of the MacDuncan clan is half gone. Rumor has it that the last two of the Stone Pack killed each other in a fight over a snow hare."

Shortly after that, they met up with a MacDuff wolf.

"My mate died, so did our pups. I couldn't take it any-more. What was the use of sticking around when I've lost my family?"

"How many in all do you think have died?" the Sark asked.

"Oh, no telling. I have heard rumors that Creakle, our gnaw wolf, still lives," the MacDuff wolf answered. He was a silver wolf and so ragged it was almost impossible to determine his age, but he seemed to have a feisty spirit. "I'd say the strongest clan right now is possibly the MacNamaras. They are close to the sea, you know. 'Tis said those wolves know how to fish, and so far the sea ain't frozen. So some wolves might have headed north and east to their territory. But I would think that we're half gone right now. I considered going that way, but I heard the Blood Watch needs some help. The thought of outclanners filling up the Beyond with their kind — not a pleasant one. And you know they are just about mean enough to survive. Don't let anybody tell you life is fair."

After this depressing encounter, the Sark and Gwynneth continued. The weather worsened, if that was possible, and although they had been heading in vaguely the same direction, they soon lost sight of the lone wolf.

It was as bitter as in the darkest days of the hunger moons. "It's cold enough to freeze a wolf's shadow," the Sark huffed, enveloping her own head in a huge cloud of breath fog. She continued to grumble as they tore apart a snow hare that Gwynneth had spotted. They licked up every bit of its warm blood and moved on.

They were now entering one of the loneliest reaches of the Beyond. But the Sark seemed to be onto something. Gwynneth sensed that the spoor had become stronger. How often she had wished that she had been blessed with the Sark's keen sense of smell, but owls' perception of scent was decidedly dull. It was their ears and their eyes that guided them. And right now, slipping through the fissures of the wind, Gwynneth detected a tiny creaking sound ahead. It sounded like a tree groaning in the wind, but there were no trees in this stretch of land. The Sark was quickening her pace on the ground below Gwynneth and appeared to be tracking toward the sound source as well.

Gwynneth began tipping her head one way, then the other, while contracting the muscles around her facial disk to scoop up sound. It was a black night with no moon, no stars. Perhaps if there had been, Gwynneth would have seen it sooner. But on the blackest of nights the blackest of trees melted into the dark void of the Beyond. The Sark, guided only by sporadic scent clues, felt like the blind wolf Beezar. Beezar was a small constellation that appeared during the spring moons. Under a starry ceiling, the blind wolf stumbled west, his front paw always raised as if fearing that with his next step he might fall off the edge of the sky. But the scent guiding the Sark was growing stronger.

"It's straight ahead, ma'am! Straight ahead!"

And then the Sark saw it, too. An Obea tree — as such trees were called by the wolves. And she knew instantly that this was where the helmet of Gwyndor, father of Gwynneth and best friend of the Sark, would be found.

It might seem odd in a sparsely wooded country that it was a tree with which the Skaars dancing had begun. But the Sark was almost sure it was so. The Obea tree, of which there were very few, was so named because it was said that only one in a thousand of its seeds ever sprouted. And then it took hundreds of years for it to grow. So it was fitting to name the trees after Obeas, the barren she-wolves charged with the task of taking *malcadhs* from their mothers and leaving them to die. Some also called these trees witch's trees for their black spectral branches that clawed darkly at the sky. The *skreeleens* told howling tales of witches when they read the lightning, the *ceilidh fyre*, that scratched the sky during summer thunderstorms. Obea trees were to be avoided, for it was rumored that even to be near them would cause barrenness. Such were the superstitions of the wolves.

"I know about Obea trees," Gwynneth protested. "But, ma'am, it makes no sense that a wolf would make a hero mark at a tree that wolves feel is cursed."

"No, it doesn't make much sense. However, I don't believe for one minute that this was the place your father died. There is a scent missing. But the helmet rested here, among these roots."

"Then what is this place?"

"It's a place where someone has been hiding the helmet." The Sark paused. "And it's a wonderful hiding place. No one wants to come near the tree for fear of being cursed by barrenness. And you see these roots? They're called buttress roots," the Sark said in an oddly distracted voice.

"What?" Gwynneth had been lost in a maze of questions as she tried to make sense of what she was seeing. She had not paid attention to the tree roots, which she now realized were rather unusual for this region.

"Buttress roots. They're like walls in a cave. They flare up to help support the tree because the ground is too hard here for roots to dig in. And the roots provide a perfect hideaway for your father's helmet. My goodness gracious!" she exclaimed. "Look at this!"

"What?"

"A cache! A rather nice cache — frozen pretty solid. A baby weasel, also a stoat. And, oh my goodness, some ptarmigan eggs! Now, tell me that a decent bird like a ptarmigan is not going to have tastier eggs than an odious tern! We've got ourselves a little feast here, my dear." The Sark paused and looked up. "But we need patience just as much as we need food."

"Patience for what, ma'am?"

The Sark's eyes narrowed. "I feel it in my marrow that if we stay here long enough, we shall meet the wolf who took your father's helmet and mask. This is his hiding place. All we need to do is lie in wait."

Gwynneth did not say anything for a long time. Then she turned to the Sark. "Ma'am, if my father didn't die here, where do you think he breathed his last?" Finding the helmet and visor was important to Gwynneth, but she wanted to know where Gwyndor died almost as much. She hoped it was a lovely spot.

The Sark spoke softly now, almost gently. "I think he died in a patch of rabbit-ear moss."

"But how — how would you know that? You wouldn't just say something to make me feel better, would you?"

The Sark's hackles rose. Gwynneth realized almost immediately that she had said the wrong thing.

"What kind of wolf do you think I am?"

"I'm sorry. I shouldn't have asked."

"When you brought me the voles wrapped in moss, it was the scent of the moss that triggered my memory."

"Yes. So?"

"There was blood on that moss — vole blood. And now it begins to make sense. There were traces of the scent of blood and rabbit-ear moss on that helmet. Your father died of a wound to his head. I assure you his head bled onto a bed of rabbit-ear moss. That's where he took his last breath and where some wolf decided to honor him."

The Sark got up now and pressed her nose to a buttress root, inhaling deeply. Then she took a step back and sniffed the ground.

"You think so, ma'am? You really do?"

"I do, Gwynneth," the Sark replied solemnly. She looked straight into the owl's dark eyes while her own spinning eye grew very still.

"Thank you, ma'am."

"Don't thank me, thank that scroom."

Gwynneth knew that the Sark, who prided herself on logic and disdained anything smacking of the supernatural, must be pained to give credit to a scroom.

The two settled into a snug little space created by the soaring buttress roots. Although Gwynneth could not help but think it would have been much cozier had it been lined with rabbit-ear moss. It was the softest moss and was often used in owl hollows, particularly when chicks hatched out. Meanwhile, the Sark was thinking how clever it was of a wolf to take the helmet and visor to an Obea tree, certain to be avoided by any other wolves.

It was a perfect place to hide a disguise used for what she was beginning to believe was a diabolical dance, a dance of submission and death. It was not a warrior who led these dances, nor was it evil incarnate — just a weak and stupid wolf. *No gall grot*, thought the Sark. Wasn't that the owl word for "raw courage"?

Toward midnight, the tree began to shake and shudder as a slashing rain pelted the branches. Ice driven by screeching wind slanted across the night. "Sounds like a pack of foaming-mouth creatures out there," the Sark commented.

It became even colder. The two animals huddled closer to each other and tried to conjure up memories of the warm snow hare blood that had coursed down their throats the day before. The meat was not the tenderest, but became more succulent in their memories.

"What's the best meat you ever ate?" Gwynneth asked.

The Sark answered immediately. "Spring grass–fed caribou. If you get them during the Moon of New Antlers, there is just nothing better. You've never tasted anything like it."

"And I don't suppose I will. They're a little out of my size range."

"Spring is the only time I run with a *byrrgis*, really."

"I never knew you went out with a *byrrgis* at all."

"Don't be shocked. I'm not totally antisocial."

"What position do you run?"

"Something middling — a packer, most often a tight end packer. Nothing spectacular like an outflanker. But when I have a yearning for caribou, I join up."

"What's your favorite food after spring grass–fed caribou?"

"Marmot."

"Marmot — really?"

"I know, most wolves find it too gamey. It's an acquired taste. What about you? What do you like?"

"Red squirrel — very nutty with a hint of winter grass. You can get them during the Caribou Moon." Gwynneth paused. "Funny, isn't it, how just talking about food sort of feeds you twice?"

"Indeed! There must be a scientific explanation for it," the Sark replied.

"I think it's just imagination. Imagination can feed you, keep you alive."

"Yes, I suppose so," said the Sark. She was thinking, however, that the imagination of the *cag mag* wolf who wore the helmet and visor of Gwyndor was becoming absolutely lethal. She recalled that faint tinge of death on the wind when it had come down from the ice cliffs. Outclanners, she had thought at the time — outclanners who would not hesitate to feed on a dead or dying wolf.

For some reason, the Sark did not believe that the wolf who wore Gwyndor's helmet was an outclanner. She was not sure why she felt this way, but she was certain. And perhaps the most frightening thing of all was that this prophet might not have any idea of the real harm he — or she — was doing. Innocence with a core of evil — could there be such a thing? Did this make the Prophet pitiable, or benighted? Did he perhaps think that he was delivering his followers from the pain of a slow death?

The Sark tossed her head. And why dancing? Dancing was for celebration and not for dying. But then again, the final act of dying known as *cleave hwlyn*, the separation at the time of death from the clan, the pack, and finally a wolf's body from its soul, was a kind of celebration, a dance of sorts, although one did not move but remained as still as possible so the soul could gently separate itself from the failing body. But was it honorable to confuse the two and divert the ritual of one to another? *It is wrong! Utterly wrong!* she thought. *Cleave hwlyn* was a deeply private act, done alone in the most solitary manner possible. It was one unique soul parting from one unique body to find its way up the star ladder with only the guidance of Skaarsgard. *It's not a* frinking *byrrgis!* the Sark silently cursed.

Did this wolf realize, the Sark wondered, that he was depraved? Well, truth be told, evil had many guises — it could seem quite ordinary, even sleep in your pack and run shoulder to shoulder with you in a *byrrgis*.

When the dawn broke, the landscape had been transformed once again. The Obea tree was clothed in a drapery of ice that sparkled so fiercely they could hardly look up into those twisted branches that writhed in glaring brightness toward the sky. Every black limb and twig was sheathed in a crystal armor of ice. But soon, as the sun rose above the horizon, it was as if a thousand rainbows had shattered in the tree, for every ice bead became a prism. When the wind blew, the colors shivered and the air flashed with pinks, reds, blues, purples, and greens in eruptions of dazzling beauty. The morning was jeweled in a phantasmagoric display of light and color.

CHAPTER TWENTY

STRANGE LIGHTS

THE LAST OF THE SUMMER MOONS was waning, and if this was summer, what would autumn bring? The last blizzard had been the worst. Faolan could not help but wonder how many sick or dying wolves were buried beneath the mountainous drifts. The wind had stopped for the moment and the swirls of snow had stilled. The Beyond had been transformed into an undulating whiteness with no separation between sky and earth. The two spheres were continuous. It was an eerie and disorienting feeling as the five wolves made their way back toward the cairns, for it seemed as if all borders had dissolved. Although they were not blind like Beezar and did not stumble, they felt as if any moment they might.

Faolan could not help but wonder if the Beyond would ever look as it once had. Would this featureless white world ever sort itself out, would the snowy blanket pull itself apart from the pale sky?

As the five friends drew closer to the Blood Watch, they spotted wolves topping the cairns. But more impressive was the sound of *skreeleens* howling. Since the five travelers had first arrived at the border between the Beyond and the Outermost, they'd heard the howlings of many *skreeleens* — many more than they would hear staying with a clan. But they quickly realized that *skreeleens* were needed at the Watch, for they were fluent in the code needed to report anything from the sighting of a caribou herd to the trespassing of territorial boundaries. On the Blood Watch boundary, they were especially valued, as it was crucial to report any outclanner movement immediately.

But now it wasn't trespassing outclanners that had the *skreeleens* howling, their marrow aquiver. Low in the milky sky, the *skreeleens* had spotted dozens of spheres of different lights in vibrant colors they had never seen. Sizzling, acid-hued globes bobbed lazily on the horizon. This spectral phenomenon had followed the ice storm of the previous night, and the *skreeleens*, who had a wealth of tales to help them interpret the sky fire of a lightning storm, were bereft of any narration for these queer orbs.

So they howled in confusion, asking the Great Star Wolf the meaning of it all.

Faolan, Edme, the Whistler, and the sisters continued to serve on the Blood Watch. Tamsen had been right about the futility of attempting to break up a Skaars circle. When the five wolves had returned, she said what they had already concluded — unless the Prophet himself could be caught, there was little hope of stopping the deadly dancing. The Whistler had quickly made himself invaluable as a *skreeleen*, howling out to alert blooders to any outclanners who had slipped across the border. Tamsen was therefore very open to the notion of sending out scouts to collect other gnaw wolves, such as Creakle and Streak.

The strange bobbing lights that had appeared so mysteriously on the horizon were having a profoundly damaging effect. Skaars dancers across the Beyond had seen these lights as a sign of the imminent arrival of Skaarsgard. They began to dance even more intensely, particularly since the Caribou Moon would soon be upon them and the star ladder would disappear from the sky, taking Skaarsgard and the heavenly constellation known as the Cave of Souls far beyond them. It was never good to die when the star ladder had vanished. Spirits were left marooned on earth and could not hope to ascend to the Cave of Souls until the constellation returned in the spring.

From the top of the cairn where Faolan was perched, he had an unparalleled view out into the night. Above the bobbing lights, the star ladder was just forming, and he could see the wolves in their palsied dance circles desperately attempting to jump for the lowest rungs. But they were too weak to make it. The Skaars dancers became more hysterical with each passing hour of the night, as the strange and luminous lights floated above them on the dark purple line of the horizon.

Below Faolan, several wolves had just collapsed, and the skulking shadows of outclanners were drawing nearer. *Have heaven and hell ever come so close together?* Faolan wondered. *Or is it all just hell?*

A cohort of blooders rushed in, but they were too late for one wolf. In a shaft of moonlight, a stain of blood spread slowly over the snow.

As Dearlea and Mhairie approached the top of the cairn, Faolan's attention was momentarily distracted.

"You're not on duty yet," he commented.

"Oh, we just thought we'd come keep you company," Dearlea said.

"Some blooders who went out hunting found two ptarmigan. So we've saved some for you when your watch is done."

"We thought it might make you happy just thinking about the ptarmigan," Dearlea said.

"Yes, it does, thanks," Faolan answered. He knew the bird was just an excuse for the sisters to come up and see him.

When they were not on watch, Dearlea and Mhairie tended to stay close to Faolan. Yet Faolan was still uncertain how they felt about what he had revealed to them.

Faolan's feelings, however, were clear. He was a member of a family. He had living sisters, he had blood kin! Ever since he could remember, there had been a small void inside him that could not be filled, not even by Thunderheart, his second Milk Giver. He had learned to ignore it, get on with life. But now that void had been filled by his sisters, and it was as if an ember burned inside him, glowing with warmth. His very marrow seemed to shimmer with this new knowledge that he was a brother — a brother to Mhairie and Dearlea. For Faolan, nothing would ever be the same again.

The Blood Watch was not as diminished as Faolan and Edme had originally thought. This was largely due to the arrival of several wolves from the renowned MacNamara clan from the northeast, the only female-led clan of the Beyond. Four nights after the strange lights appeared in the sky, two more MacNamara wolves arrived for duty on the Blood Watch. As they came up the trail toward the jagged ridge that was spiked with watch cairns, Edme recognized them almost immediately.

"Airmead! Katria!" she howled. The other Blood Watch wolves were more than pleased to see these new arrivals, for they knew the two she-wolves were highly regarded lieutenants in the MacNamara clan.

A few minutes after Katria and Airmead's arrival, a group of wolves had crowded into the rather small *gadderheal* of the Blood Watch. Tamsen, the captain of the watch, greeted them.

"Welcome. Words can't express how happy we are to see you. We are stretched thin, and if it had not been for the Namara's generosity in sending us wolves, we would truly be in trouble." She nodded her thanks to Brygeen and Oona, two stalwart MacNamara lieutenants.

"We are here to serve," Katria said. Then she turned to Brygeen and Oona and spoke. "You can go back now. More of us are coming, and I'm sure your families will be happy to see you."

Oona stepped forward. "We have not been here as long as some. Tamsen, how long has it been since you last saw your mate in the Blue Rock Pack?"

"Not since the Moon of New Antlers," Tamsen answered.

"Then you should go back, Tamsen," Brygeen said quickly. "We have two more MacNamara wolves on their way."

"You are too generous."

"No, not at all," Oona said. "Your pack needs you. This terrible thing — this Skaars dancing — is spreading. It's more deadly than any famine, and only strong pack leadership can stop it."

Despite her thinness, Oona was a strikingly beautiful black wolf. Faolan and Edme both noticed that she did not use the words "clan leadership." The Blue Rock Pack was only a pack in the MacDuncan clan, and Tamsen was only an outflanker. Not a clan chieftain. Had Liam gone *by-lang* yet again? Was the clan truly without a commander? Then it struck Faolan: Was it possible that Liam, who had never been a natural leader like his father, had been seduced by the Skaars dancing?

It was decided that Tamsen and Greer, a *skreeleen* whose voice was nearly raw from howling alerts about trespassing outclanners and wolf eaters, should be relieved of their duties after the additional MacNamara wolves arrived. Tamsen and Greer were strong MacDuncan wolves, and the MacDuncans — the Clan of Clans — was tottering on the brink of collapse and needed every good wolf it could get.

CHAPTER TWENTY-ONE

AN OWL ON A MISSION

HIS NAME WAS TULLY, AND HE was a double-chawed Great Snowy Owl dispatched from the Great Ga'Hoole Tree on direct orders. His mission was to assess the condition of the wolves of the Beyond and to see if support from the Great Tree could be of use. He was also supposed to figure out where in hagsmire Gwynneth was, as she seemed to have vanished.

Tully did not feel up to the job at all and hoped against hope that he would find that frinking Masked Owl. He knew he could never equal Gwynneth's knowledge of the Beyond and its wolves. Wolves were just plain weird.

Tully had started regretting his mission from the moment of takeoff. The weather was completely miserable. He thought he had outflown an ice storm that had been forming over the Sea of Hoolemere, but it had caught up with him. His wings had begun to ice up just as he left the Shadow Forest, and he was forced to light down on some Glaux-awful icy cliff that his talons could barely grip. Then, on the next leg of his flight, there was no place to land but the ground, on top of a drift. At least with his hollow bones and the spread of his talons, he didn't sink in.

The only good thing was that there seemed to be a few snow hares about, and, listening carefully, he could detect the pitter of deer mice. If wolves weren't so picky about what they ate — all that ridiculous big game — they might not be starving now. Rodents and snakes were perfectly good food. Did everything have to be so big and bloody and so hard to bring down? *Wolves must*, Tully thought, *expend more energy than they consume.* Or so it seemed to him. But then again, what did he know about the ways of wolves?

So far, there had been no sign of Gwynneth, nor could he spot any trees. Tully wasn't sure which he regretted more. Another night roosting in some un-owlish spot was not appealing. Alighting in a drift was hardly inviting. Snow was pretty from the air, but sleeping in it, on it, beside it, or whatever was not fun. It was cold. How did Gwynneth stand this place? Tully wondered. Well, she was a curious bird, that one.

Tully was high and skimming some cirrus clouds that stretched out across the night sky when a draft carried another noise to his ears. It was almost as if the wind ached with the sound. He banked steeply to begin a fast spiral down and was soon hovering over a bizarre sight. There was a circle of wolves flat on their backs. Their legs were extended and they were pawing the air, no, not the air, the sky — as if they were . . . were what? Searching? Reaching for something?

The words they were howling in their thick wolf brogue were almost unrecognizable, but they were begging, begging for someone to come back. *Skaars? Skaarsgard? Who in hagsmire is Skaarsgard?* thought Tully.

These wolves were in trouble, Tully realized, even close to death. The thought of them dying in this Glaux-forsaken country stirred his gizzard.

The wolves lay with their eyes rolled so far back in their heads that only green crescents showed. They were muttering unintelligibly, but every now and then Tully caught a word or two — "Skaars . . . Skaars . . ." It was a guttural cry.

"Skaars? Who is Skaars?" Tully asked repeatedly. But none of the wolves had the strength to answer. There were perhaps eight wolves in all, and one had died the moment Tully alighted. The other seven seemed to be very close to catching their last breaths. Tully was suddenly aware of a slight ticking sound beneath the snow. Pure instinct surged through him, and he plunged deep into the white drift. Great Glaux! These starving wolves had collapsed on top of a virtual treasure trove of snow mice! Half a wingspan down or less was a maze of tiny tunnels used by snow mice and most likely shrews. Very shortly, Tully had killed two rather plump snow mice and was diving down again for the clutch of babies. *No use leaving orphans!* Tully thought.

Tully was careful in his butchering. He gave each rodent a quick stab to its cranium to kill it and was careful to make sure that as little blood escaped as possible. Then he surveyed the surviving wolves. It made sense to try and feed the least weak of the wolves first in case the others were too far gone to help. So, taking the biggest of the mice in his talons, he settled next to a large gray male. First he fanned the gray with his wings, trying to stir him into some sort of consciousness.

When the gray's eyes fluttered a bit so that the green became more than just a thin crescent, Tully spoke. "I've got something here for you to eat, mate. Now, don't you go refusing it." He gave a quick stab to the life-giving artery at the base of the mouse's neck. Tully pressed the small furry creature to the wolf's mouth as the blood spurted, and squeezed the mouse.

"Drink!" Tully snapped. "I'll hear none of this nonsense about rodents. Rodents are perfectly good nutrition."

The eyes of the wolf flickered open. A shadow of consciousness glimmered in the green.

Tully chattered on in a calm, cheerful voice. "Come on, old fellow. Drink up now and I'll strip the meat for you, just the way we do for the little owlets at home. Tender to the bone, this critter is. And I'll gut him for you as well. Might have a bit of summer grass left in him. Then again, it wasn't much of a summer, was it?"

The wolf took in a bit of meat.

"Skaars . . ." rasped the wolf.

"Skaars? No. Tully's the name, fella."

"I . . . I . . . I know you're not Skaars, but did he come? The Prophet said so."

"The Prophet? What are you talking about?" Tully asked.

"The Prophet, the dear Prophet? He was here a moment ago before . . . before . . ."

"Before you passed out?" asked Tully.

"Passed out? Oh, never! I was merely in a Skaars

trance. He will find me and bring the ladder here to earth and the Cave of Souls as well."

I've pulled myself a real nutter on this one, Tully thought. What in the name of Glaux was this wolf talking about? He was completely *yoicks*. "Have another sip of blood, old fellow," Tully said amiably. He squeezed the last drops into the wolf's mouth. "Now I'm going to tend to your mates, but I'll set this mouse here. Try to eat it if you have the strength. But if you don't, I'll come back and strip some more meat from him for you."

"But what about the Prophet?"

"The Prophet. Uh . . ." Tully hesitated. Should he say he didn't know *racdrops* about any frinking prophet or should he play along? "Uh . . . I'm sure he'll be here in a jiff."

CHAPTER TWENTY-TWO

THE OWL AND THE GNAW WOLF

TULLY WAS ABLE TO REVIVE ONLY two of the wolves. The rest died. The two who had survived walked off on wobbly legs with nary a word of thanks or a look back. The Snowy shook his large white head.

"No good deed goes . . . oh, what is the saying?" muttered a voice from behind Tully.

Tully spun his head around and blinked at the ash-colored wolf.

"How you owls do that always amazes me."

"Do what?" Tully asked.

"Spin your head about like that."

"It's the extra bones in our necks." Tully cocked his head to the side. "You're not one of them, are you?"

"A Skaars dancer! What, you think I'm *cag mag*? And would they ever let a gnaw wolf join them? Not on their pathetic lives!"

The wolf began limping down the slight escarpment, and Tully noticed that he was missing a forepaw. "Who are these wolves?" he asked. "You say they were dancing? I don't understand what's going on."

"Nor should you understand. It's too bizarre, too grotesque, unnatural, absurd." The wolf paused. "Do you have any word to add to the description of that ritual?"

Tully blinked. "Who are you?" he asked.

"Creakle's the name. Gnaw wolf for the MacDuff clan. But those two, I believe, are the last survivors of the clan. And all that's left for me is to try and fend off the scavengers."

"Shouldn't the others have stayed to help you at least?"

Creakle sighed. "They're *cag mag. Yoicks* in your language. Crazy. They don't care about the dead ones left behind. In their twisted minds, they actually don't think of them as dead. They think of them as saved by Skaarsgard and of themselves as unworthy of his attentions. So they will go on dancing until they die, too."

Tully tipped his head and looked at the gnaw wolf, blinking rapidly.

"Confused, confounded, astonished, bedeviled?" the wolf asked.

My, he has a large vocabulary, Tully thought. It seemed to be Creakle's habit to use long strings of words to suggest a single idea, but every word he spoke did describe Tully's mental state.

"Yes, yes, all of the above," Tully replied. "But who is this prophet? I heard them all mumbling about him as they were dying. One or two of them even thought I was the Prophet."

"Yes, in their delirium I can see how that might happen — it's the shape of your face."

"What?"

"He wears the helmet and visor of an owl — a guardian, perhaps from the great tree."

"What! I can hardly believe it."

"Believe it! I've seen him."

"But do you know who he is?"

"No. I have my suspicions and I've tried to track him, but he's clever. He never leaves scent marks, and in this famine, all of our scent marks have become quite faint anyway. So it's difficult."

Creakle continued, "I'm heading north now, north and west to the Blood Watch. Now, that's a real job. There are rumors that my old friend the Whistler has distinguished himself and is now a lieutenant of the Blood

Watch. Imagine that! A gnaw wolf becoming a lieutenant. I'll tell you, there are some blessings to this famine."

"Do you know Gwynneth?" Tully asked.

"Of course. Who doesn't know Gwynneth!"

"Well, then, have you seen her?" Tully persisted.

"Not for a while. There are rumors that she moved her forge."

"Might I travel with you to the Blood Watch? My mission was to report on the condition of the wolves and find Gwynneth. But so far I've had no luck on the Gwynneth front. And as for the wolves . . ." He looked at the bodies of the six dead wolves in the snow. "Well, I'd like to be able to report something more positive."

"I would find your company most satisfactory, pleasing, gratifying. It would gladden me, delight me, indeed tickle the cockles of my marrow."

Cockles of his marrow? Where does he get these expressions, these words? It suddenly struck Tully that this poor gnaw wolf had had no one to talk to for so long that he'd had to save up all his words.

"Aah," Creakle said, "I can see that you are a bit perplexed. I think I've mixed my metaphors here. Cockles and marrow. Cockles are a bivalve mollusk. Gnaw wolves eat those, too — river clams. Most wolves won't touch them. I have even gnawed their shells. We gnaw wolves — amazing lot, aren't we?"

But what was most amazing, Tully realized minutes later when he was flying above Creakle, was how beautifully this pawless wolf moved through the snow. The deep drifts seemed to part for him as he loped north and west. Plumes of snow fanned out from either side of his path, as if he had sprouted gigantic wings. For a moment Tully forgot that Creakle was a wolf at all, but thought he was looking down on some mythical creature. *Great Glaux*, he thought, *what am I seeing?*

CHAPTER TWENTY-THREE

A Significant Encounter

YES, GWYNNETH THOUGHT AS SHE looked at the sleeping Sark, *we can see more perfectly in the dark than almost any animal, and yes, we can twist our heads nearly all the way around, and we can fly so silently, and yet . . .* She tipped her head to regard the Sark's muzzle with wonder. *What that wolf can smell!*

With only two little holes in her nose, the Sark was able to know that the Prophet had been to the place where Gwynneth's father had died. The Sark in many ways knew more about and certainly had a longer history with Gwyndor than Gwynneth did. Did Gwynneth envy the Sark? In some ways she did. Gwynneth's mother had died shortly after she had hatched, and her father didn't have the time to raise her. So he had taken Gwynneth to the owl she knew only as Auntie, the Rogue smith of the

Silverveil. Gwynneth couldn't have asked for a better teacher. The Great Snowy had learned her craft in the Northern Kingdom from the legendary blacksmith Orf on the Island of Dark Fowl in the Everwinter Sea. But although Auntie was a wonderful caretaker, Gwynneth couldn't help feeling jealous that the Sark knew things about her father that Gwynneth didn't. She could almost hear her auntie scolding: *Envy is the worst of all sins. To be envious is to be cursed, to be blind to your Glaux-given gifts. Envy is trouble. Envy gets you nowhere in life!*

I better get unenvious real quick, Gwynneth rebuked herself. She heard the Sark sigh in her sleep, almost sweetly, as if she were having a deeply pleasant dream. Was she dreaming? Did wolves dream? It seemed an impractical activity for a practical creature such as the Sark.

Gwynneth dreamed when she slept, but it was nighttime now — time for an owl to be awake and flying. Gwynneth did not particularly care for the schedule they had fallen into, but she supposed it worked well. She could be abroad at night keeping a sharp lookout for the Prophet, while the Sark could keep watch during the day. So Gwynneth took one last look at her sleeping companion and stepped out from the buttress roots to lift off into the air.

It was a cold, windless night, perfect for flying, as the air was dense. *It's like flying on the downy*, Auntie used to say. The downy was a reference to the soft feathers an owl has beneath its tougher exterior ones. When chicks hatched out and finally dried, they were clad entirely in down tufts. She had just spread her wings to lift off, when the Sark awoke.

"Your second flight tonight, I think. I never realized owls had so little patience," the Sark said.

"It's not a question of patience. It's being cooped up on this — this — this vigil or whatever you call waiting in these roots for some lunatic wolf to show up in my father's helmet."

"He'll come, just give him time. You yourself said that the Skaars dancers are more active than ever now."

"Yes, but the Prophet's not there. So far, I haven't had a glimpse of him." Gwynneth sighed. "And when we do find him, what exactly do we do?"

The Sark's head jerked with new attention. "Why, we get your father's helmet and visor back and restore it to its rightful place — to wherever his hero mark was made. We shall force this wolf to tell us where exactly that is. And in the process we can expose this fool, unmask a false god, and stop the dancing."

"Can you be sure?"

"No, of course not. No one can ever be sure of anything."

"Why do you think the dancing has increased, ma'am?" asked Gwynneth after a small pause.

"Now, that's a good question. I have a theory. Those odd lights that have been appearing for the last several nights have somehow incited the dancers. I think they feel it is some sort of sign that Skaarsgard's arrival on earth is imminent." She paused. "Poor fools."

"But, ma'am, what do you think those lights are? I myself find them . . . well . . . eerie."

"Spook you, do they?"

Gwynneth cast her eyes down and nodded her head. She was somewhat embarrassed to admit that they did.

The Sark continued in a much gentler voice. "Oh, Gwynneth, don't worry. They are nothing more than air — an atmospheric phenomenon similar to ice halos. As the sun sinks below the horizon, ice crystals caught in layers of cold air act like prisms and bend the sun's rays. We are seeing them now because, although the weather feels fiercely cold like winter, the sun still rises and sets on its summer schedule. In the winter we don't see such a phenomenon because the sun is at a different angle to the earth. It's as simple as that!"

It did not seem at all simple to Gwynneth. Nevertheless, she took solace in the Sark's dispassionate explanation. But what was the explanation for the growing madness of the wolves of the Beyond? Gwynneth and the Sark had estimated that fully half the wolves were caught up in the strange cult of Skaars dancing. The sights that Gwynneth had seen as she flew over this territory near the Outermost seeped into her dreams and clung to her feathers like cobwebs. She could not rid herself of them. And the knowledge that the Sark had tried to protect her from — the fact that wolves were eating other wolves — had been revealed to her one night as she flew over a circle where the last Skaars dancer had collapsed. Wolves wild eyed and reckless had melted out of the shadows. They had not even waited for the dancing wolves to die but began dismembering them as they still breathed.

It was all too horrifying for Gwynneth. She had flown into the savage wolves' faces, batting their paws, and even lost one primary in her attempts. It was not a severe injury. She would molt that feather come spring — if spring ever came. But her fight had proved useless.

She had returned to the Obea tree determined to say nothing, but the Sark smelled them on her. Smelled that Gwynneth had tangled with a wolf-eating wolf.

"Don't, Gwynneth, don't!" the Sark had said somberly.

"Don't what?"

"You know, dear. What they're doing is unspeakable. But you can't stop it." The Sark had squeezed her eyes shut. Her voice broke. "I couldn't stand to lose you, Gwynneth. Don't do anything foolish. Now let me see about that feather."

That had been the end of their discussion. They never spoke of it again.

The clear patch appeared in the thickly clouded night sky, and a few stars gleamed down upon them. Gwynneth spread her wings to take flight.

"Be careful!" the Sark cried out.

Gwynneth spun her head almost entirely around to look over her tail feathers. "Don't worry, ma'am."

But the Sark's words of caution frightened her. It was so unlike the Sark to say good-bye in this fashion. Gwynneth was not fearful for herself but worried about this new, somewhat gentler Sark. It was so uncharacteristic of her to fret about Gwynneth's safety.

Gwynneth had not flown far when she saw two plumes of snow rising from the ground. They were slightly uneven, like the mismatched wings of a bird. There was only one wolf who ran like this — the gnaw wolf Creakle. If Faolan was the swiftest runner, Creakle was certainly the most beautiful runner in the entire Beyond.

"Gwynneth!"

At the cry, Gwynneth swerved in flight. "What in the name of Glaux," she muttered, and then saw Tully melt out of a cloud bank.

Creakle had slowed to look up. "Here, land on my back, you two. The snow is awfully deep," Creakle called.

The two owls alighted on Creakle's withers. Gwynneth noticed they were very thin, but of course it was supposed to be summer and wolves shed their thick undercoats in the summer moons.

"Creakle!" Gwynneth exclaimed. "I am so happy to see you — see that you are alive. I have wondered how you gnaw wolves are doing."

"Some better than others. Tearlach died."

"Oh, no!"

"But the Whistler is, so far, still alive, and rumor has it that he's with Faolan and Edme at the Blood Watch. That's where we're headed. The Blood Watch is in poor shape, and they need all the help they can get."

"Faolan and Edme are at the Blood Watch!" Gwynneth was shocked. "How could I not know this? I've been camped so close with the Sark."

"Is that where you've been?" Tully exclaimed. "The Great Tree sent me to find you. You have been absent, gone, vanished, unaccounted for, missing in action, Gwynneth!" He caught himself. He was picking up Creakle's penchant for synonyms. "The tree is none too happy. They need you now, they need an owl who knows the Beyond."

Gwynneth cocked her head. "I'm sorry, but let me tell you what's happened."

"Please do," Tully said somewhat huffily.

"You know about the Skaars dancers, right?"

"How could we not know about them?" Creakle asked.

"And the Prophet?" Gwynneth asked.

Creakle and Tully nodded.

"Do you know what that stupid prophet wears to hide his identify?" Gwynneth asked.

"I've heard a mask of some sort," Creakle said.

"Not just some sort. The Prophet wears the helmet and visor of my father."

There was a long silence.

"What?" Tully squawked.

"Gwyndor's mask?" Creakle asked.

Gwynneth nodded.

Gwynneth explained how they had found the helmet and visor's hiding place and how sooner or later the Prophet would come back to it. "So you see, I have to return to the Obea tree and stand watch with the Sark. I had no idea Faolan and Edme were so close. It's close as the owl flies but not as the wolf runs, and you can bet that no wolves come near that tree. That's why it's perfect for concealing something. Can you two continue on to the Blood Watch and tell Faolan and Edme what the Sark and I have discovered?"

"Of course, of course!" Both the owl and the wolf nodded.

"And if the Blood Watch can spare them, perhaps they might come." Gwynneth hesitated. "I mean, who knows what we're up against with the Prophet. There is only so much an elderly wolf and one owl can do. And for Glaux's sake, don't ever tell the Sark I called her elderly!"

Gwynneth paused. Another thought came to her.

"Tully, I've introduced the Sark to rodents — rodents as nourishment."

"Yes, I introduced — or tried to introduce — mice to the Skaars dancers. They were too far gone for it to matter."

"But not everyone is a Skaars dancer — certainly not yet. You could be of great service. Catch rodents. You know where to look for them." Gwynneth paused. "You could bring them first to the Blood Watch and then to the wolves at the Ring of Sacred Volcanoes. If the owls want to help, that's the best thing they could do."

Then Creakle spoke. "Tully, could you fly back to the Great Tree and get other owls to join you?"

"The search and rescue and the tracking chaws would be perfect for this. Yes. I'll help. I'll leave now. I saw a place where there might be voles. I'll hunt them down for the Blood Watch and then fly east to the Ring and on to Ga'Hoole."

And so it was decided that Creakle would continue on to the Blood Watch and report to Faolan and Edme what Gwynneth had told them.

CHAPTER TWENTY-FOUR

THE BEAR'S DEN

FAOLAN AND EDME HAD JUST come off the Blood Watch when Creakle arrived. What the gnaw wolf told them was astonishing; Edme had to ask him to repeat the entire story.

At the conclusion of his tale, Faolan turned to Edme. "I don't see that we really have a choice. We can't let the Sark and Gwynneth face the Prophet alone."

"No, I don't think we can. And now Creakle is here, so at least that's one wolf to cover for us while we're gone."

Faolan frowned. "I think we have to go immediately. I hate the idea of the Sark and Gwynneth alone in this situation. I fully believe that this prophet is as dangerous as any foaming-mouth wolf. Look how this dancing has spread — like a disease!"

The wind was with them and they were able to go at a press-paw pace. They had been traveling for a few hours when Faolan perceived a familiar reverberation deep beneath the snow under his splayed paw. That paw was unusually sensitive to anomalies of the ground and could sense when a stream flowed under a thick crust of ice, or a maze of mice runnels coursed beneath a hardpack of snow.

"Stop!" he called out to Edme, who had taken the lead. She turned around.

"What's the matter?"

"Nothing really, but . . . it's hard to explain. I think — I think there are lava beds beneath these drifts."

"So?" Edme asked. Faolan had begun to dig in with both claws.

"Faolan," Edme complained, "you aren't really planning to dig down to some lava beds. I mean, whatever for?"

Suddenly, Faolan's paw struck rock and there was a hollow *kah-kah* sound.

"You see, I'm right — lava beds!" He was extremely excited.

"Faolan, I'm not following you at all. We're supposed to be on our way to the Sark and Gwynneth at the Obea tree."

"No! We have to stop here." His hackles rose and stood rigidly.

"But why?" Edme implored. "Why must we stop here?"

"I spent my first winter in a lava tunnel, with Thunderheart. It was our winter den. There's a tunnel beneath us and a way into it not far from here. It's the entrance to someone's den. We have to find it."

Edme tilted her head to one side so her single eye could study her friend. There was an urgency in his eyes that told her this wasn't simply about Thunderheart. There was something more going on.

"Edme," Faolan pleaded. "There could be bears in there and they could be in trouble."

"How can you tell?"

"I . . . I feel it in my paw."

Edme looked down at Faolan's splayed paw, the one that condemned him to be a *malcadh*. She knew that his paw sometimes could feel things other wolves' paws could not. It was not entirely unlike her single eye that sometimes saw more than two eyes could.

A cloud scudded across the moon, temporarily darkening the lonely landscape, and then there was a flash of silver. It was Faolan, leaping in an immense arc to land on what looked like snow. Suddenly, the entire world seemed to erupt in a snarling cacophony. It was as if all the wolves of the Dim World had been unleashed. A splash of blood spurted into the night, then another.

Edme bounded toward the snowdrift where Faolan seemed to have disappeared.

"Great Lupus!" she exclaimed when she found herself not in a drift at all, but at the entrance to a lava cave. A cub was squealing, bleeding from one ear. Two wolves stood cowering by the black lava wall, and a mountainous form could be seen beyond them. The wolves were obviously outclanners. They had the smell of dead wolf upon them and would soon have carried the scent of dead cub as well. Wolves of the Beyond lived in harmony with the bears, much as they lived in harmony with owls. Outclanners lived in harmony with no animals, not even their own.

"Mama! Mama, wake up." The huge mother bear slept on, but Faolan jumped to attention. He reared up on his hind legs, towering over the outclanners. One of the wolves had a gash across his face. The other trembled in Faolan's shadow.

Then there was an enormous bellowing yowl.

It's happening again, Edme thought. Faolan's muzzle

had lengthened into a boxy shape and his claws looked twice their regular size. Faolan flung the wounded outclanner against the wall, killing him instantly. Then, with a quick flick of that strange paw, he ripped open the belly of the other wolf. The wolves were dead in just seconds. Blood pooled on the floor. The cub, a female, whimpered inconsolably. And as peculiar as Edme thought Faolan's transformation had been, what happened now was even more mystifying. He had seemed to slip back into his old pelt, but only partway. With the lumbering gait of a bear, he approached the cub, making oddly soothing growling sounds. He picked up the cub ever so gently by his mouth, settled into a corner of the cave, and cradled the cub in his two forelegs, just like a mother bear!

Faolan, what are you? Edme thought. *What in the name of Lupus, Glaux, or the great bear Ursus are you?*

CHAPTER TWENTY-FIVE

"The Prophet Shall Reward You!"

"WELCOME TO OUR HUMBLE ABODE!" the Sark said. "Take no offense, but did I smell you coming? It smells like you had a tussle with some wolves and a bear."

"No offense taken," Faolan said wearily. Edme had waited for Faolan to offer some explanation, but he remained silent.

"Uh —" Edme began, "we came across a cave with a grizzly and her cub sleeping."

"False hibernation. I've been expecting this to happen, what with this weather," the Sark answered quickly.

"Yes." Faolan nodded. But he seemed reluctant to continue.

Edme realized that the less Faolan said, the better. If he had not been aware of his odd transformation at the

Skaars circle, he was aware of this one. "There was a bit of a tussle. We had to step in to drive out the outclanners and wake up the mother bear. So here we are."

Gwynneth stepped forward. "Creakle filled you in?"

"Yes," Faolan said. "We couldn't let you try and face off with this *cag mag* wolf alone. He must be exposed."

"And even then," the Sark added, "there is no telling if this will stop the Skaars dancing."

"You're right," Edme said. "But we have to try."

Faolan turned to the Masked Owl. "This is a terrible insult to your father, Gwynneth. For a wolf to disturb a hero mark, to wear your father's armor — it's unimaginable."

"For an owl to even have a hero mark is so extraordinary!" Edme exclaimed.

"Is it?" Faolan asked.

"Is what?" Gwynneth asked.

"Is it strange for an owl to have a hero mark?"

The Sark, Gwynneth, and Edme looked at Faolan in astonishment.

"Faolan — have you ever once heard of an owl for whom a hero mark was made?"

Faolan's eyes grew dim, as if he were reaching far back in his memory. "No, no. I suppose you're right." But he did not sound very convinced.

So the three wolves and the owl drew up a plan. Gwynneth would continue her night flights to scout for the Prophet as well as any game in the area. During the day she would rest, and Edme and Faolan would strike out on scouting expeditions.

The Skaars dancing circles were spreading, but there still hadn't been any sign of the Prophet. However, they soon picked up increasing talk of his arrival. Faolan and Edme no longer attempted to break up the circles. It seemed quite useless. But if outclanner wolves were hanging around, they chased them off. And when they found small game, such as snow hares, and at one point a beaver, they brought it to the starving dancers. The oddest thing was that the Skaars dancers never seemed to be that hungry. Faolan and Edme wondered if the dancers' stomachs had shrunk, for they would often vomit up the meat.

"I don't think it's their stomachs," Edme said one day when they had found a rare ptarmigan and brought it to a circle.

"What is it, then?"

"I think it's their minds. Something's happened to their minds."

"No, no good wolves!" said a voice from behind them. Faolan and Edme wheeled around to find the speaker, a pathetic-looking gray male of indeterminate age. This wolf was so thin, it was hard to look at him. He seemed to have but a single tooth in his mouth and they could see every rib through his thin pelt.

"You think we are hungry, but we are not. You think we are thin, but we are fat in our souls. You look at me and say, 'Oh, poor creature.' But you are seeing my flesh, blood, and fur, not my soul. When the Prophet comes he will, as he promised, bring the star ladder right here to where I stand." The other dancing wolves had stopped dancing to press around him.

Edme was tempted to yell at the gray wolf, to tell him that he was a perversion, an insult to everything valued by honorable wolves, an insult to the Great Chain, even. But she steeled herself and held her tongue. The important thing was to find out if there was a chance of catching the Prophet. "And when do you think the Prophet might come?" Edme asked mildly.

"Very soon."

Just then, a relatively plump mouse trotted by. Faolan slammed down his paw on it, killing it instantly.

"Now, here, one of you should eat. You, sir," he said,

shoving the mouse toward the gray wolf who had begun the conversation with them. But the wolf shrank back and so did the others.

"Oh, no!" He spoke vehemently. "The Prophet must not find us fat or our souls will not be ready for the ladder. Leave it instead as an offering for the Prophet."

As he approached, Edme and Faolan could hear a scraping sound as if his bones were rubbing against each other inside his pelt.

Faolan and Edme stared in astonishment.

"But surely the Prophet doesn't eat? He must want to be prepared for when Skaarsgard comes with the ladder."

There were soft huffs from the other wolves. The gray wolf turned to them and shook his head. "Be gentle with our friends. They do not understand yet."

"What don't we understand?" Faolan asked.

"This food, this dead mouse, will be transformed and become spirit food in the presence of the Prophet. It will feed his soul and thus all of our souls. It will feed him so he might complete his work on earth."

"And where should we leave it?" Edme asked calmly, as though this wolf's explanation was the most sensible thing in the world. Faolan shot her a glance as if she had gone *cag mag*.

"There by that rock. It's a whispering rock. It will be safe there and we shall send out the message. He will come. He always does."

Faolan and Edme exchanged glances. This was their chance to see the Prophet, to lure him out and stop the dancing. They could only hope the mouse was tempting enough. If it could bait the Prophet, it might be worth it.

So Faolan and Edme set the dead mouse on the rock, then watched while a white wolf nearly as thin as the one they had been speaking with came and began to scratch out a message with his claws.

"Thank you," the Skaars dancers said before resuming their dance. "The Prophet shall reward you."

The dancers were weak now. As one began to collapse, another called out, "Oh, his soul is becoming more radiant! Oh, his spirit stirs so beautifully!"

"How soon will the Prophet come?" Edme asked the wolf with whom they had been speaking.

"The Prophet is to the south, we believe. The wind is from the north . . . so . . ." He was so depleted he couldn't finish the thought.

We have time! Edme and Faolan both thought. A bit of time was all they needed.

Faolan and Edme could not wait to get back to the Obea tree and tell the others. They needed to rest and to consume the remainder of the food the Prophet had cached in the tree roots. Everything depended on their being strong enough to catch him when he came. The Skaars dancing he had started was killing more wolves in the Beyond than the cold or the famine. It had to be stopped.

When they returned, the Sark was up but Gwynneth was already sound asleep, although the sun had barely risen.

"Back so soon?" the Sark asked.

"We found something," Edme said. "Nearby."

"Yes, smells like a mouse — a little fatty. Where is it?"

The two wolves explained.

"Spirit food!" the Sark snorted. "Oh, how nourishing! I feel myself chubbing up already. About to split my pelt! What a racket this prophet has going. What a frinking — to borrow an owl expression — racket!"

CHAPTER TWENTY-SIX

The Prophet Comes

THE PROPHET HAD HEARD THE MESsage. Spirit food awaited him. But he had just been leading circles to the south, and it had been a long night. He needed to get back to the Obea tree, to rest, to think about things. The helmet had rubbed a raw spot just beneath his ears where the visor slid down. He needed rest and he needed the lovely stoat that awaited him.

Occasionally he had doubts about eating when he told his followers not to. But, he was leading in the only way he could. He gave his followers not the will to live, but the grace to die beautifully and then be reborn. He had discovered his gift when the herds vanished. The lack of food had cleared his mind, leaving him with the ability to understand the workings of the celestial. On a night when he was so racked with grief that he thought of hurling himself from a cliff, the stars had called out to him. Not in words but with a deep resonant thrumming. He had looked up and seen light falling through the star ladder with Skaarsgard dancing on its rungs. The light began to throb and his own heart beat in harmony with the light above. That was the moment he realized his own significance in the great drama that was about to occur in the Beyond. It was not a famine; it was a deliverance, and he would lead it. He began to lift his feet one at a time, then quickened the steps. "I am the one! I am the one! The Prophet who will help Skaarsgard bring heaven to earth, soul to marrow, and marrow to soul!" He looked down and saw his body truly for the first time. It was but a vessel destined for decay, and a vehicle through which the true spirit is released.

Now when he ate, it was only to keep the vessel whole until the final fracturing, when his work and Skaarsgard's would be complete.

The Prophet knew himself to be a container for light — all the light that poured from the sky. It suffused him, illuminated his marrow, guided him so he could guide the wolves of the Beyond to their true destiny. He tipped his head back now and felt the helmet shift. The visor slipped back and he scanned the sky. But enormous thick gray clouds had moved in from the west and sealed the sky. He searched for the tiniest rip in the gray, just a crack to show the sun rising in the east. Ah, there it was! He felt a ray strike the visor and he flinched. He tipped his head to lower the visor once more.

CHAPTER TWENTY-SEVEN

The Visor's Glint

WHEN THE SARK AWOKE, SHE SAW that Gwynneth was still asleep, as were Faolan and Edme. Gwynneth was squashed into what looked to the Sark like a very uncomfortable position. The Masked Owl slept in an upright posture in the V where two sides of the buttress roots met. "Well, to each her own," the Sark mumbled to herself. She got up and noticed that Faolan and Edme must have gone out hunting earlier, for there were two voles left out. The Sark had to admit that she had acquired a taste for these rodents, as had the other two wolves. They had also become proficient hunters of the little creatures. Although the Sark stopped just short of pronouncing rodents delectable, they certainly could be most satisfactory. Bats were less so. But still, in these times beggars could not afford to be choosers. And the

Sark made no mistake that they were all beggars in the Beyond.

The Sark's mind drifted to the Skaars dancers. They were begging for death. Something had killed their hope as surely as water on a flame.

The Sark wandered over to look out from their root shelter. The shelter faced west, and she saw something that flashed in the distance. *It can't be the sun*, she thought. The sun rises in the east. But it could be a reflection! A reflection of the rising sun on metal! The Sark had seen it once before in the Slough: a glint on a helmet, on a visor. *Finally!* she thought. *The Prophet is coming!*

"Gwynneth! Faolan! Edme!" the Sark whispered.

The owl's eyes flew open and the Sark gently but firmly clamped Gwynneth's beak in her mouth. "Don't hoot! He's coming. Don't make a sound, any of you!" She unclamped Gwynneth's beak and nodded to the west. The sun was reflecting off of the helmet at such an angle that all they could see was a growing radiance that did not look like an animal at all. Nevertheless they felt his presence. *Who is this wolf?* Edme thought, and felt a quiver deep in her marrow. Finally, a great evil was about to be revealed.

Faolan felt a tremor pass through him as he also realized they were about to come face-to-face with a creature of great power. A creature who had cast a deadly spell on the poor starving wolves of the Beyond.

The flashes were becoming larger and still the Prophet was a faceless being, a creature from an unknown place. To feel him so strongly was unnerving.

The wolf was close enough now for the Sark to pick up his scent. He looked vaguely familiar to all of them, but only vaguely. If he would just take off his helmet! Just then, he seemed to sense their presence. The fur on his ruff rose in a stiff frosted nimbus gilded by the rising sun, as if Great Lupus himself had fallen to earth. The Prophet looked like a god, not a wolf — *a false god*, the Sark thought.

"Now!" the Sark said. Gwynneth darted into the air. The three wolves raced out from behind the roots.

The Prophet squeaked and turned to run. Gwynneth folded her wings and spiraled down directly into his face in a kill plunge, but he reared up, batted her aside, and leaped ahead into a dead run with Faolan and Edme at his heels. Although the Prophet was thin, he was fast. Faster than any wolf they had seen in the Beyond for the last two moons. He had energy, a maniacal energy that did not come from meat. His speed showed the zeal, the ardor of a fanatic.

Edme cut behind the Prophet to come up on his flank. It was a turning guard maneuver, but it wasn't working. Faolan tried to run harder, but a sudden shift in the wind smacked him squarely in the face. The Prophet ran in the lee of a line of drifts that blocked the wind at least temporarily. The gap between them widened, and if the Prophet could stay in the lee of the drifts, he could run even faster.

Urskadamus! Is everything against us? Faolan swore silently. But hadn't that always been the way, he thought suddenly. Hadn't he been put out on a *tummfraw* as a newborn pup? Hadn't that icy *tummfraw* broken loose in the flood of a raging river? And yet he had held on with his tiny claws and survived. He would hold on now. He would claw his way through this wind.

He felt his legs stretching out. The splayed paw punched through the windy drafts. He could tell that the wolf felt him bearing down and he saw the Prophet waver, then cut to the side to get closer to the line of drifts. *I can read his every move. He has no cunning.*

Had this wolf never run a *byrrgis*? Every time the wolf hesitated, Faolan picked up on it. The wolf's indecision was Faolan's advantage and he used it for all it was worth. The fight had come down to not strength or energy, but strategy. Faolan swerved in deeply. He was now in the windless tunnel in the lee of the drifts and he felt his legs stretch out. But the Prophet was still ahead of him and disappeared around a bend. When Faolan charged around the bend, the Prophet had disappeared. Dread flooded through Faolan, and he skidded to a halt. How could it be? How could the Prophet have disappeared?

At just that moment, there was an explosion of snow from the ledge above Faolan. In the vortex of swirling white, Faolan saw eight legs scrambling, kicking against the empty air.

Suddenly, Faolan realized four of those legs belonged to Edme. Her single green eye glittered like a beacon in the tumult. The Prophet must have sprung onto a snow ledge in one last desperate effort to get to the top of the drifts, and now he and Edme were falling toward the ground. A question flashed through Faolan's mind. *Where did Edme come from?* But there was no time to think.

"Flank port!" Edme cried out as she landed and began to chase after the Prophet.

She was packing the gap — as she had with the moose. Faolan once again joined the chase, cutting in on an angle. Edme came in on the opposite side, and they slammed the Prophet's hips at the same time, throwing him off balance. The Prophet rolled. Faolan was on him in a second, pinning him to the ground. Gwynneth flew straight down at his face, using her talons to flip back his visor.

"Liam MacDuncan!" she screeched. The helmet fell off and began to roll down a short bank.

"My helmet! My helmet!" cried out the chieftain of the MacDuncan clan.

"*Your* helmet!" Gwynneth screeched again in the blistering cry of Masked Owls. "That's my father's helmet. It's Gwyndor's!"

The wolf blinked. His green eyes were bright with a kind of moral emptiness, the dark pupils at their center like dead beetles. Gwynneth could not help but think that had this creature been an owl, his gizzard would be *kerplonken* — dead. The two wolves who had brought him down could see that he was a wolf who had been severed from his marrow.

The Sark, who had fallen behind on the chase, now stepped up to snarl over him. "Try dancing now, you fool!"

The wolf was shaking so hard he could barely speak, "I . . . I didn't mean to —"

"Mean to what — steal my father's helmet?" Gwynneth shrieked. "Disturb the only hero mark ever made for an owl? Trample the grave of a warrior? Is that what you didn't mean to do?"

"I meant . . . I meant —" the wolf stammered.

"You meant nothing," the Sark barked at him. "You misled your clan and others. You are a weak fool."

"I meant to give hope!" the Prophet protested.

This enraged Faolan. He began pounding Liam's chest with his powerful splayed paw. "You call hope the 'spirit food' the dancers leave for you while they starve?"

The Sark, her eye twirling and pelt twitching, spoke. "Faolan is right. Don't speak to us of hope. That's not hope you offered — that's despair. Are you too stupid to know the difference? You think putting on the armor of a truly valiant hero and begging for death is hope?"

Liam MacDuncan started to say something, but the Sark thumped a paw down over his muzzle.

"I'll give you death!" she howled. "But you'll die alone with your despair. Was that it? Was the despair too much for you to contain within your own pathetic mind? You wanted to share it! That was the only way you could become a leader. But you're no leader, and no chieftain. Great Lupus, your father must be crouching in the Cave of Souls with his tail between his legs and his ears laid back in shame! He must be cringing in our heaven!"

"Don't!" cried Gwynneth, for she saw the Sark bare her long fangs to rip into Liam's neck. "Don't! He's the only one who knows where my father died. He must take us there."

"I will, I will," Liam MacDuncan mewled like a whining pup pulled from his mother's milk. The sight was so sickening that Gwynneth yarped up a pellet.

The fever of anger seemed to drain out of the Sark. She looked at Faolan, Edme, and Gwynneth, and swallowed. In a small, barely audible voice, she said, "Yes, your death must wait. This goes beyond a single wolf, one crazed wolf. Don't you see?

"I have always been a lone wolf but within the steady little universe of the Beyond. Yes, I have looked askance at many of the elaborate rituals and codes of the clan wolves, but Liam!" The Sark turned to the quivering wolf. "Liam MacDuncan, you came from the oldest and most venerable clan in the Beyond. It was the clan of the original Fengo, the founder of the Watch at the Ring of Sacred Volcanoes. And now you have come to this. What a perversion you have created. You've lured wolves to their deaths with this insane dancing. It must stop now! Do you hear me?" Her voice rose. "It must stop! We are in the worst of times, and you have found none of the courage in yourself that has been in the MacDuncan marrow for over one thousand years. You have helped bring us to the brink of complete and utter ruin." The Sark paused, and her head dropped. "The stench of ruin is all I smell!"

CHAPTER TWENTY-EIGHT

Too Late

THE OFFICERS OF THE BLOOD Watch gathered in the *gadderheal* along with Mhairie and Dearlea. Faolan and Edme flanked Liam MacDuncan, and the Sark stood at his hindquarters. Gwynneth stood apart with her foot on her father's helmet.

"What is this about?" Tamsen said, staring at Liam. "And why have you brought the helmet and visor of your father, Gwynneth?"

"You recognize them, Tamsen?" Gwynneth said.

"Of course I do. I was but a youngster at the time, but I fought in the War of the Ember. But it was my understanding that because of Gwyndor's actions in that war, a hero mark had been made for him. And the helmet and visor were never to be moved, on the direct orders of the great Duncan MacDuncan. Your father, Liam."

"So they were," Liam answered.

Gwynneth's black eyes widened. *It was true and Liam knew of it!*

"So why are they here? What is the meaning?"

"They are here because I have abused the dignity of my office as a chieftain of an ancient and honorable clan. I . . . I deluded myself in thinking that I could save the Beyond. I tried to call down Skaarsgard and . . . and . . . and I believed that I had to become — was meant to become — a god on earth, a prophet."

A profound silence fell upon the *gadderheal*. "*You* are the one?" Tamsen barked. "*You* are the wolf who began the despicable dances and you used the helmet and visor of Gwyndor for your crimes?"

Liam didn't utter a sound, but hung his head in shame.

Tamsen whirled around to face the other wolves. "As captain of the Blood Watch, I invoke the privilege of the Sayer and I say this: The wolf Liam MacDuncan, false-marrowed and deceitful, must be taken to as many dancing circles as possible between here and the Ring of Sacred Volcanoes and unmasked. The fraud that he is must be revealed. We shall stop this dancing once and for all!"

For the first time in many moons, Faolan, Edme, the two sisters, and the Whistler raced with real hope to a large dancing circle. There were perhaps a dozen or more wolves gathered on a high plain. The five friends felt their hearts beating wildly in their chests as Liam MacDuncan walked stiff legged toward the Skaars dancers. At least four of the dancers were already falling to their knees.

"Go to the ones still dancing," Gwynneth hissed. Liam walked forward.

"Regard me," he croaked in a hoarse voice to a swaying dancer. She stopped in her steps.

"The Prophet!" she sighed in near ecstasy.

"A false prophet!" Liam said this forcefully, and then slowly but with great deliberation tipped his head, so the visor slipped back and revealed his face. The she-wolf cocked her head to one side and stared at him blankly.

Her mate nudged her. "Keep dancing, dear." He did not even seem to register that his prophet was the wolf Liam MacDuncan, even when he removed the helmet and it rested in the snow beside him.

"It's as if they both still see the helmet and visor on him. They don't see his true face!" Edme muttered in disbelief.

A thin little pup rushed up to the ragged pair. "Mum, Da, that's just a wolf, not a prophet at all. It's Liam MacDuncan! I saw him once. He's just a wolf."

But his parents did not even hear him. They did not even turn to look at their pup. "Mum!" the pup whimpered. He scampered up to his mother and tried pulling her tail. "Mum, listen!" But she shook him off as she might shake off a burr that had stuck in her ruff.

"The pup is coming with us," Faolan said abruptly. "I am not leaving him here to die." He turned and looked at the dancing circle. "This is despicable. This is a living *tummfraw*!"

The words exploded in the silence of the Beyond.

Faolan dipped down and gently picked the pup up by his ruff in the manner that very young wolves were carried. As they walked away, the little pup looked back, but a fog bank had descended and swallowed up his mum and da. He tried not to whimper. He tried to remember that it was not so long ago that his mum had played with him by the river before it was locked with ice, when the water flowed. She had promised to teach him to swim and to fish when summer came. But summer never arrived and now his mum and da were gone.

The wolves walked on. They would demand no bones of contrition from Liam. They would take him to no more circles. It was too late. The Skaars dancers were beyond rescue, lost in their trance. What had started out as a famine had rotted into a perversion, a disease of submission, an addiction to death. The very spine of the Beyond quivered, as if the marrow were leaking from its bones.

CHAPTER TWENTY-NINE

GOOD-BYE TO FRIENDS

THE WHISTLER ACCOMPANIED Faolan, his sisters, Edme, Liam, the pup, and Gwynneth for the first few leagues after the Skaars circle.

"You'd better go back to the Blood Watch now," Edme said, turning to him. "We're sorry to leave you, but we have much to report to the Fengo. He knew nothing about the Skaars dancing when we left." She glanced at Liam. "But with the arrival of the MacNamara wolves, at least we can tell him that the Blood Watch is stronger."

"And," Faolan interrupted, "we will tell the Fengo about you, Whistler, and your service to the Blood Watch."

"I would be dead if it weren't for all of you," the Whistler replied. "You saved me. The Blood Watch is a good place for an old gnaw wolf."

"They need everybody, no matter their rank," Faolan said. "There's no time for abuse."

"Abuse is an indulgence if we are to survive," Edme said acidly. Faolan looked at her with surprise. Edme, generally sweet and optimistic, had become somewhat of a cynic.

"I'll miss you, Whistler," Dearlea said, stepping forward with her tail tucked firmly between her legs and her ears laid flat. Her sister was soon beside her and both began to grovel on the ground in the standard submission rituals.

"Mhairie, Dearlea! For Lupus' sake!" the Whistler exclaimed. "Didn't you just hear Edme? There's no time for such nonsense."

"Who knows what makes sense anymore," Mhairie said, twisting her face up so she could speak.

"Dearlea, Mhairie." Faolan spoke gently but firmly. "Get up now. Give the Whistler a proper good-bye and we'll be off." Faolan went up to nuzzle the Whistler's ruff, and his sisters followed.

"That's more like it," Edme muttered.

The Whistler watched as the wolves headed east. The night closed in on them, and the strange lights began to bob in the twilight on the horizon. He could see the silhouettes of other wolves beginning to form circles for their relentless dance of death. He was tired of it all — wolves begging Skaarsgard to come fetch them, the wolf eaters, the desperate howlings of confused *skreeleens*. He had endured abuse all his life, and yet for some reason, he had never given up hope that someday he might distinguish himself and be selected for the Watch at the Ring of Sacred Volcanoes.

A full lifetime of abuse had never caused him to give up hope. How ironic it was that now, in the midst of a famine, he had never been happier. Yes, he was hungry like everyone else, but he was treated better since he arrived at the Blood Watch than ever before. Tamsen had once abused him, and now seemed to regard him with a new light in her eyes. She had appointed him second *skreeleen*, which never would have happened back in the old days in Blue Rock territory. Despite the hole deep in his throat, everyone knew that the Whistler's howling was melodious and possessed exquisite clarity and power. His alert calls could be heard all the way down the line.

And he was honest. When all the rest of the *skreeleens* were howling about the peculiar lights, making up stories as they went, he refused. When Tamsen pressed, he had told her there were no stories for these lights.

"They have no history," he'd said. "And there is no way to interpret them as with the sky fire of summer storms. It would be dishonest for me to howl in complete ignorance."

Tamsen respected him for that. "You must do what you feel is right, Whistler," she'd said.

Had a distinguished outflanker ever spoken to a gnaw wolf in this way, the Whistler wondered. No. And this gave hope to the gnaw wolf with the twisted throat.

The Whistler was a lieutenant now, and there was even talk of making him captain. It was miraculous really, when one thought of it. As long as he showed up for his watch, howled his share of alerts, and joined in a skirmish when required, the rest of the Watch officers were pleased. Not once since he arrived had he been head-butted, nipped, or rolled, as gnaw wolves were usually treated. The ranking system of the Blood Watch was based on merit and not dependent on ancient notions of superiority of blood lineage that had very little to do with accomplishment. Order and respect were maintained purely through a wolf's ability to execute the task at hand. Some wolves couldn't stand it and seemed to silently break down, as Caila must have, going *by-lang* to join the Skaars dancers.

Sometimes there was a slight indication that a wolf of the Watch was on the brink of going *by-lang*, certain physical signs. A wolf's pelt is made up of two coats — an undercoat and an overcoat. The undercoat is composed of very short fur and keeps a wolf warm. The wolves grow thick undercoats in the fall for winter and begin to shed them in the spring or early summer. Most of the wolves had kept their thick coats through this summer in response to the prolonged cold. But the wolves who were about to go *by-lang* began to shed rapidly. Because they grew colder and could not keep any heat in their bodies, they grew hungrier as well.

The other sign was a cloudiness in their eyes. Although a wolf's night vision is not as good as an owl's, they can see quite well in complete darkness. At the very back of their eyes is a tiny mirrorlike membrane. The Old Wolf word for it, which had persisted, was *scathan*. In wolves about to go *by-lang*, the *scathan* became fogged and could no longer reflect light. Wolves also have another membrane that slips over the front of their eyes, like a second eyelid, to protect the eye from dust or debris. This eyelid often ceased to work, so that some wolves began to stumble about like Beezar, the blind wolf constellation. It was a sad thing when it happened.

CHAPTER THIRTY

Back at the Ring

"WE HAD HEARD OF THIS INSANE dancing," the Fengo said. "But I couldn't believe it was true. And you are telling me that Liam MacDuncan was leading it?" He swiveled his head around and stared darkly at the shamed wolf. "Are the clans truly diminished by half?"

"Perhaps even more than half," Edme said. "Creakle has reported that he is possibly the last of the MacDuffs."

"Creakle, the MacDuff gnaw wolf, the last of his kind?"

"We had to bring back this little pup," Faolan said. The pup was eating a vole that had been brought in just before they arrived. He had taken readily to rodents on their journey to the Watch.

"He's a bit of a miracle, I would say," the Fengo whispered to himself.

"He's learned to eat mice — owl food. I think it saved him."

"It's saved us!" the Fengo said.

"How do you mean?"

"The owls — the Rogue colliers, the Rogue smiths have been bringing us rats and what have you. But one owl in particular has been quite helpful."

"Who might that be?" Gwynneth asked.

"A Snowy Owl — Tully is his name."

So, she thought, *Tully came through.*

As the other wolves left, Finbar motioned for Edme and Faolan to come closer. Mhairie and Dearlea lingered.

"Sisters, wait outside for a moment. I know all this is difficult for you," the Fengo said.

Mhairie stepped forward. She glanced briefly at Dearlea, who nodded and seemed to encourage her to speak. "Sir," she began hesitantly. "As you have been told, our second Milk Giver has rejected us. Our clan is in such disorder that we cannot, we do not, want to return to it."

"Of course not. What would you think of joining the MacNamara clan?"

"The MacNamaras!" The sisters' green eyes flickered with excitement.

"Yes. But I have many things to consider, so be patient for now."

"Of course, of course." The sisters nodded.

When they left, the Fengo turned to Faolan and Edme. "I would never have sent them back to the MacDuncans."

"Thank you," Faolan said. "Without Caila, Mhairie and Dearlea will not have much status with the MacDuncans, not these days. And they are both smart. Mhairie is an outflanker and Dearlea was training to be a *skreeleen*. But you need a mother, a high-ranking one, to ensure these things." Faolan paused. "But, sir, there is something else about my sisters."

"What is that, Faolan?"

"Whether they join the MacNamara clan or not, I need to take them to the *drumlyn* I built for our mother, Morag. I need to show them her bones on the end of the Broken Talon Point."

The Fengo looked up, his eyes bright. "That is a wonderful idea and you've certainly earned the privilege. I think you should leave immediately. There seems to be a blessed pause between blizzards. We've had some luck of late with snow hares, and there are of course several more voles. Speak to Jasper. There should be enough food to give you a bit of energy for the trek."

Faolan turned to leave, but the Fengo called to him. "And by the way, Faolan, tell your sisters that yes, they should go to the Namara and ask to become members of the clan. It makes such good sense. After all, it is the clan your mother, Morag, joined at the end of her life and it's not too far beyond Broken Talon Point, where her bones rest."

"I'm sure they'll be very happy."

As soon as Faolan had left the *gadderheal*, the Fengo swung his head toward Edme.

"Edme, you have not inquired about Winks."

"I . . . I . . . am afraid to."

"Yes, I thought you might be. My dear, she died a few nights after you left."

"Yes, I felt it." Edme's muzzle quivered. "At least it was before the Caribou Moon, and the star ladder was still shining. The star wolf could point the way for her."

"Yes, indeed." Finbar paused. "I was with her when she died, Edme. She passed with such dignity, such composure. Never begging for Skaarsgard like these fool wolves. She just slipped away. I could almost feel her soul glide from her pelt, her paw slip into that of Skaarsgard."

"How lovely," Edme replied.

"Now, there was a wolf of the order!" Finbar tipped his head and shut his eyes. The words "a wolf of the order" constituted the highest compliment one could pay a wolf of the Beyond. A wolf of the order lived with effortless grace within the sanctity of the Great Chain that linked the wolves to all the elements in the universe between heaven and earth.

"And, Edme." Finbar's voice quickened.

"Yes, sir."

"She spoke of you as she left."

"She did, sir?"

"She did indeed. She said that she loved you, Edme. She loved you like a mother loves a daughter."

From the top of her cairn, Edme saw Faolan and his sisters approaching. "I can't leave my post right now. Can you come up?"

"Yes," Mhairie called.

The three wolves scrambled up to where Edme was perched.

"We just want to say good-bye." Dearlea tipped up her head.

"I won't be gone long," Faolan said. "The Fengo has given his approval for my sisters to join the MacNamara clan."

"You take care, Faolan," Edme said.

"I will, and you, too. Don't let Banja get you down. You know she's just a cranky old thing. Likes to make trouble."

"Oh, don't worry about that," Edme said almost dismissively. "I can take care of Banja."

This was a new Edme, Faolan thought. Along with that new slight tinge of cynicism came confidence.

They nuzzled each other's ruffs. Then Edme turned to Mhairie and Dearlea. "You be good to Faolan. He's my best friend in the whole Beyond."

"He's our brother!" both girls said at once.

Faolan's eyes filled with tears. Mhairie came over and nudged him playfully. "You know, I wonder who was born first. Because if I'm the oldest, I think I get to be the boss, don't you?"

"Well, I think we'll never know," said Dearlea. "And I'm not sure it matters because, Mhairie, you were just plain born bossy, no matter if you were first, second, or third."

Faolan turned to Edme. "I understand that you, too, are here only for a few nights."

"Oh, you heard about that?"

"Yes, Twist told me that Finbar wants you to lead a

small group to bring in any starving wolves to the Ring. Thanks to the owls, there are enough rodents to feed them — at least for now."

"Yes, at least for now," Edme repeated, her voice subdued.

Faolan immediately wished he could take back his words, for they conjured up too many dreadful questions about the future, about their futures. He was almost afraid to look into Edme's eye, which saw so much. Could she see the fate in store for them?

Edme put a paw on his shoulder. "Try not to worry too much, old friend," she said softly. She turned and then sprang into the first of a series of scanning jumps. When she was at the peak of her jump, she howled to the three wolves below her.

"Good-bye! Good-bye, dear friends!"

CHAPTER THIRTY-ONE

The Musk Ox

FAOLAN AND HIS TWO SISTERS traveled in a companionable silence for three days. As the sun sank behind the horizon, casting a green glow over the land, Dearlea stopped abruptly. "What are those four sticks?" Ahead of them four sticks of exactly the same size appeared to have been deliberately planted in the snow.

"They aren't sticks! They're legs!" Faolan said. "Musk ox legs!"

The three wolves bounded forward. They quickly realized that the musk ox, an elderly female, had been caught in an avalanche. Had she been younger, the herd would have helped to dig her out. But because she was ailing and slowing their travel, they had apparently abandoned her. It was not cruel on their part at all. The musk ox would endure more pain attempting to keep up with the herd than falling into a frozen sleep. For the three wolves, it was an unbelievable piece of luck. Not only would there be enough meat for the three of them, but there was enough to feed the entire Carreg Gaer of the MacNamara clan. So they would at least arrive with some good news.

Digging down to the body was hard work, and it was even harder to tear through the thick, coarse mat of guard hairs and the soft underfur to get to the meat. The musk ox had apparently died only a short time earlier, because her blood was not yet cold and her meat was still soft.

Faolan cautioned his sisters to eat slowly. "It can't be good to eat this much meat when we have been hungry so long and living on small creatures."

"Well, at least it's warm," Mhairie said as she bent her head over the steaming pile of meat. This gave Faolan an idea. He knew they were not far from Broken Talon Point and the coast of the Bittersea. But the wind coming off that water sounded different from what he remembered. It sounded like wind driven across a frozen sea. There was absolutely no shelter on Broken Talon Point, and the warmth they had gained from nourishing themselves would drain out of them faster than they could imagine. If they could keep warm, the food in their stomach would fuel them for longer. Faolan peered at the huge cavity of the musk ox stomach from which they had dragged her entrails.

"We should sleep here," he said, looking at his sisters.

"What do you mean by here, exactly?" Mhairie asked suspiciously.

"I mean right here." He nodded at the ripped abdomen of the musk ox. "It's as big as a small whelping den. We can fit easily and we'll be warm."

Dearlea and Mhairie looked at each other, then Dearlea spoke. "One thing, Faolan." She turned to look at her sister.

"It's not a bad idea, Dearlea," Mhairie replied.

"No, it's a good idea," Dearlea said.

"Well, then, what is it?" Mhairie pressed.

"There is nothing noble in eating an animal that's already dead. So even though we didn't kill this musk ox, we need to perform *lochinvyrr*, for she will have given us both nourishment and shelter."

Lochinvyrr was the ritual that wolves followed when they brought down an animal. As the animal was dying, they would gaze into its eyes. Prey and predator would lock gazes as if something were being agreed upon between the two. It was a demonstration of respect in which the predator acknowledged the life it was taking. The wolf would sink into a submissive posture as if to acknowledge the greatness of the gift the dying animal was giving, while with great dignity the dying animal seemed to say, *Yes, I am valuable. My meat will sustain you.*

The musk ox's eyes were glazed with ice and she stared dumbly into the night that now sparkled with stars, but still the three wolves gathered round her and began to lick the ice from her dead eyes. Soon enough the starry roof of the night was reflected in the musk ox's eyes, and Faolan, Dearlea, and Mhairie bent down on their knees while grinding the sides of their heads into the snow. They fixed the ox in their gaze and performed the ancient ritual of *lochinvyrr.* When it was complete, they crawled into the bloody cavity of her abdomen and slept.

When they woke several hours later, the copper disk of the sun was trembling on the horizon.

"Still hungry?" Faolan asked.

"No, not really. I ate my fill last night," Mhairie replied.

Faolan had not yet told his sisters about the *drumlyn* he had built for their mother. He had not found the right words.

The sisters knew that their mother had spent her last days with the MacNamara clan. But that was all they knew, really. They weren't aware that after she had been driven from the MacDuncan clan and her two healthy pups taken to be raised by Caila, she had found a new mate in the MacDonegal clan, where she'd had a brilliant career as an outflanker. Morag had led a worthy life and Faolan had been determined to honor it in the only way he knew how — by building a *drumlyn*.

For a wolf like Faolan, it was instinct to gnaw a bone not just for meat, but to incise it with beautiful carving. The instinct was imprinted on his very marrow. The first time he had ever carved a bone was long before he had even joined a clan. He had been a lone wolf and brought down a caribou by himself. The caribou was a worthy opponent — old, weak, but very clever — and so Faolan had honored her with a *drumlyn* made of her bones. He had dragged her body more than a league and fought off ravens the whole way in order to place her bones near the river on a high bank where they could remain undisturbed. He had found the same sort of place for the bones of his mother. It was close to the tip of Broken Talon Point, and he had planned to head there first and then on to the MacNamara clan with his sisters. But now that they had found the musk ox, he knew they must go first to the Namara, the clan chieftain, and tell her where to find the meat.

"I had planned to take you first to the *drumlyn* of our mother."

"*Drumlyn?*" Mhairie asked.

Then Dearlea spoke up. "Is that one of your Old Wolf words, Faolan?" The sisters were used to Faolan blurting out Old Wolf words and even bearish expressions.

"I suppose so. I used it before I had ever heard the word 'cairn,' which is what wolves call a bone mound."

"So . . ." For once, Mhairie's tongue seemed to stumble in her mouth. "So you got her bones and . . . and —"

"Morag's bones were not ready to be carved yet. I first found other bones to tell her story on, and since then I've made two trips back. Our mother's bones are beautiful."

He read the slight confusion in his sisters' eyes. For them, bones were carved to inscribe laws, to honor the Great Chain that ordered the wolf world, or to chronicle events. That was all. The notion of memorializing a wolf through bone inscription, especially one that was not a clan chieftain but just an ordinary wolf, was difficult for them to grasp. Furthermore, for Faolan to call the bones "beautiful" was eccentric to say the least.

But to Faolan, the bones of his mother were beautiful — they were lustrous with a pale gray patina. The knurled ends of her femurs rose and fell like waves in a stormy sea. Her skull seemed to shine with a blinding white — all of her bones were lovely. Faolan stepped closer to his sisters. Their fur was stained with blood from gorging on the musk ox, but he caught the golden flecks in their eyes. "You want to know about your first Milk Giver, don't you?" he said softly.

"Oh, yes," they answered, although it seemed more like a sigh in the air than actual words.

"I'll take you to her *drumlyn* and show you the story of her life. But first we must go to the Namara."

They were standing on the edge of the Broken Talon bight. Normally they would have had to swim across it and follow the coast to get to the Carreg Gaer of the MacNamara clan. But while the waters of the Bittersea churned with gales, the bight was protected from harsh winds and had frozen solid. They could run straight across it, saving a great deal of time.

They were across the bight before high noon, and a short time later, two MacNamara scouts came racing toward them.

"We thought you were musk oxen!" exclaimed the first, a large brown male wolf, skidding to a halt. The other scout blinked at them, for their fur was stiff with blood and they reeked with the scent of the musk cow.

"Faolan, is that you?" the second scout asked.

Faolan dropped the curved horn of the musk ox he had been carrying for his mother's *drumlyn.*

"Yes." He quickly explained about the creature caught in the avalanche. And with their pelts spangled with frozen blood and hoarfrost, the three wolves trotted after the scouts into the encampment of the Carreg Gaer of the MacNamara clan.

Idiot! Idiot wolf! The words kept up a din in Gwynneth's brain that she thought could almost be heard by the Sark and Liam on the ground below her. They were following the cowardly wolf on the trail to Gwyndor's hero mark, to the place where he had died and his bones were resting.

"We're getting near!" The Sark tipped her head up to call to Gwynneth, who was skillfully navigating through the thick trees of the Shadow Forest.

"Yes, we are. How can you tell?" Liam asked.

"I can smell the rabbit-ear moss," the Sark replied.

"Oh, yes, I forgot about your keen sense of smell," Liam mumbled.

"You forgot more than that, you idiot!" Gwynneth called down. She was wearing her father's helmet and visor now.

A quarter of an hour later they arrived at Gwyndor's grave and Gwynneth lighted down. "So this is the place?" she asked.

Liam nodded. There was an immense blue spruce tree and even Gwynneth could smell the spicy rabbit-ear moss that crawled partway up its trunk. The moonlight filtering through the boughs of the spruce was tinged a silvery blue and cast a pool of lovely light. *This is a nice place to die*, Gwynneth thought as her dark eyes filled with tears. "And his bones —" Her voice broke.

"In the hollow," the Sark replied, nodding toward a cavity in the tree trunk not far from the ground. "I can smell them."

"My father wanted them as high as possible off the ground. That was as far as he could reach," Liam said in a small voice. "He didn't want any animals to disturb the bones."

Gwynneth and the Sark whipped around to glare at him.

"Rather ironic, isn't it, that his own son was the one he had to guard against," snarled the Sark.

The Sark felt the softest whisper of a breeze stir across the withers at the base of her neck. She looked up. Gwynneth was hovering up near the spruce's top branches, gently nestling her father's helmet into the highest hollow in the tree. In her beak she held a bone — one of the fourteen vertebrae in an owl's neck. They had nearly twice as many vertebrae as most animals, as she was fond of pointing out. When she had finished safeguarding the helmet and the bone in the new hollow, she alighted on the ground. "I'm going to take every single one of these neck bones and put them way up there." She spun her head about quickly. "Then Da can keep watch over his hero mark!"

When Gwynneth had completed this task, she perched on a branch just outside the hollow. She looked up through the interlacing branches silvered by the light of the moon. She would wait patiently, she thought, wait for Auntie's scroom. As she caught the first glimpse of a vaporous mist float down through the branches, she began to *wilf*.

Splendid, whispered a voice that was not quite a voice. *Splendid, dear!*

CHAPTER THIRTY-TWO

The *Drumlyn* of Morag

"SO HERE WE ARE," FAOLAN SAID quietly. "I built it here because there is a good view of the Ring of Sacred Volcanoes, and on a clear night when I am on watch, I can see Broken Talon Point from my cairn and imagine that I can see the *drumlyn* of our mother."

The lashing of the winds off the Bittersea had stripped snow from the *drumlyn.* The bones were clearly visible, looming pale in the moonlight. They seemed almost transparent, and it crossed Dearlea's mind that they could have been made from crystal.

"Dearlea, are you cold?" Faolan asked.

"No, no. I just . . . I can't explain." Then very softly she said, "Mum?"

"She died very peacefully, Dearlea. And Brangwen was a good mate."

"It's too bad that we didn't get to meet him," Mhairie said.

On their arrival they had been told that Brangwen had left for the Blood Watch a few days earlier.

"Can you show us Thunderheart's bone?" Mhairie asked.

"Well, if you really look I think you'll see it."

"That one!" Mhairie said, touching her nose to a huge bone at the base of the *drumlyn*.

"Yes, her paw bone." It was one of the largest bones in the *drumlyn*. "I had buried it on a slope near the salt lagoons in the Slough. I retrieved it about six moons ago to bring here."

"I can see the carving you did. It's so beautiful!" Dearlea said.

"It's the story of our time together — the summer we spent fishing on the river, the fall, and then our winter den." He paused. "Would you like to carve a bone for Morag?"

The Namara had diligently kept watch over Morag's bones as her body decomposed. She had even posted a guard to protect Morag's remains so that Faolan could come back for more bones to add to the *drumlyn*.

"But what will we say? We never knew her," Mhairie said.

"Tell her about yourself. She was an outflanker, Mhairie, and so are you. And, Dearlea, you had been selected to be a *skreeleen*, to read the *ceilidh fyre*. You have much to inscribe. Stories that a mum would be proud of."

"Are you going to carve any more?" Dearlea asked.

"Not tonight. Now it's your turn."

Faolan knew he shouldn't carve while his sisters were trying to incise their own stories. Watch wolf carving skills were vastly superior to those of ordinary clan wolves. It would only make Mhairie and Dearlea anxious if he were to gnaw beside them. "There's a shelter in the lee of the point. I think I'll go there for a rest. But you begin your bones. It will feel good, I promise."

"We're not nearly as skilled as you, Faolan," Mhairie said.

"But your story is yours, and yours alone. You are the only one who can tell it to our mum."

"Our mum," Mhairie repeated, savoring the words on her tongue.

And Faolan's sisters began their stories. At first their incisions were stiff and rigid, blunt marks staccato in their rhythms.

Mum. They named me Mhairie. Was this the name you chose? I grew up to be an outflanker, like you, only not as good. Mum, you should know that Caila took good care of me — Mhairie stopped. Should she write about Caila's rejection? Faolan said that one must never lie on a *drumlyn* bone. So she began scratching lightly with her incisors. *Until the famine sickness came upon her, she took very good care of us*. And now the marks flowed like small ripples in a river touched by wind. *Dearlea and I think something happened to her marrow. She said we were not her daughters. She rejected us. And I suppose she was right. She was not our first Milk Giver, you were. But she raised us as if she were our true mum. We never felt she loved us less than any other litters. She loved us and took care of us until the famine sickness came upon her. She was so proud of me when I became an outflanker and when Dearlea was chosen to train as a* skreeleen. *She was a proud mum.*

Faolan was more tired than he'd thought, and while his sisters carved, he fell into a deep sleep. In his dream he carved as well. Bone that was slightly familiar. It was a twisted femur, and he couldn't understand why he felt he'd come across it before. He loved that bone, but it wasn't his mother's, nor was it Thunderheart's. It was a wolf bone, not a bear's.

I was a bear, he said in his dream.

He felt a deep thrill surge within him. Suddenly, it was as if he had been transported back to the Cave Before Time. He could feel those walls that seemed to breathe with life surrounding him, the animals pounding across the rock face of the cave. He could hear their panting and see the spiraling painted marks on the stone, just like the dim tracery on the pads of his splayed paw. *I am so close*, he thought, *I am so close to the answer, so close to the heart of a secret — my secret. What is it?*

Not yet! Not yet! a dream voice whispered. And once more the spirals from the cave walls that matched the marks on his splayed paw emerged from the mists of Faolan's dreams and reminded him that he was but part of a larger design. *I was not born for death and yet I have died a thousand times*, he thought. *And now I am born again for these hard times.*

His marrow began to boil and his dream split, as if a bolt of lightning had cracked open his skull. There standing beside him was another wolf, a paltry creature so old it looked as if his legs would not support him. A tattered pelt hung over stick-thin bones that seemed rimed in frost.

I was not born for death and yet I have died a thousand times, the wolf echoed.

Faolan jolted awake. "Who said that?" he asked. Those were the words from his dream, from the frost wolf. Faolan got up and walked to the mouth of the den to look out. He saw his sisters working diligently on their bones. On the edge of the wind, he could feel a deeper cold coming. It was now almost fall. What would the hunger moons of winter bring?

Faolan looked up at the sky. The stars blurred, as if the constellations were stumbling toward a precipice, like Beezar the blind wolf. There was but one thought in Faolan's mind:

My service is not over. I am in but my first pelt of a new season. Can this be so?

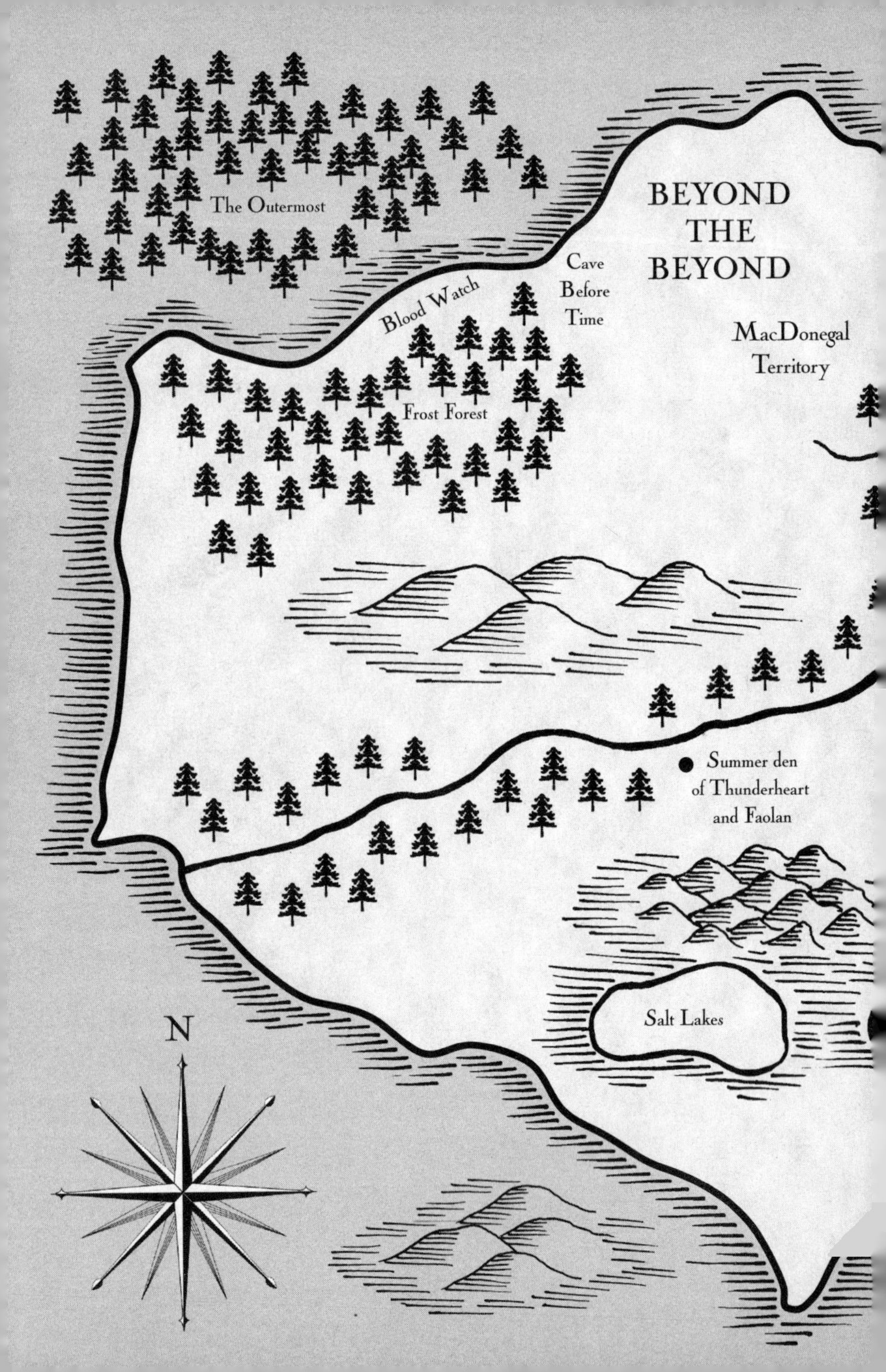

The Outermost
BEYOND THE BEYOND
Cave Before Time
Blood Watch
MacDonegal Territory
Frost Forest
Summer den of Thunderheart and Faolan
Salt Lakes
N

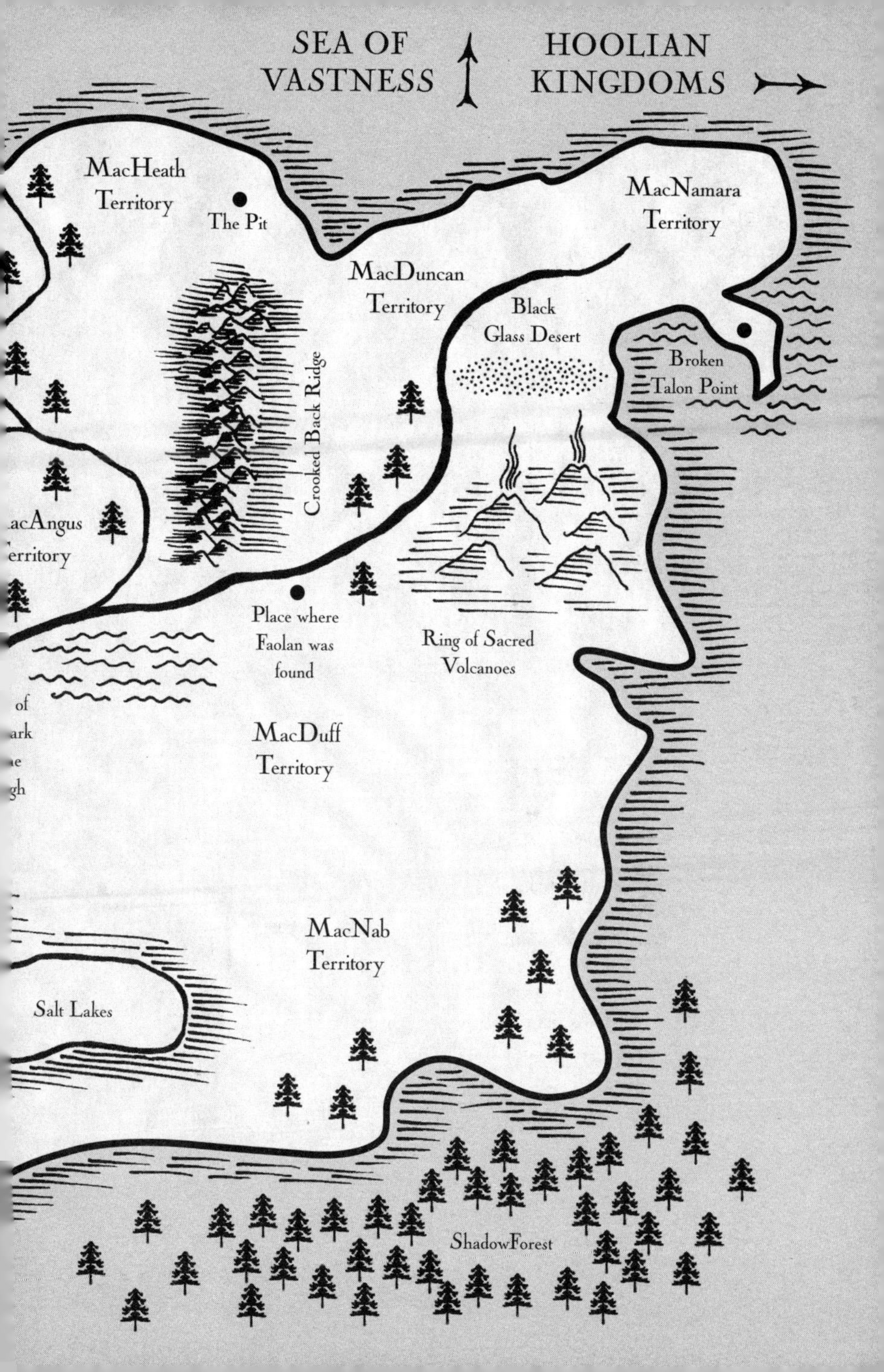

SEA OF VASTNESS
HOOLIAN KINGDOMS
MacHeath Territory
The Pit
MacNamara Territory
MacDuncan Territory
Black Glass Desert
Broken Talon Point
Crooked Back Ridge
Place where Faolan was found
Ring of Sacred Volcanoes
MacDuff Territory
MacNab Territory
Salt Lakes
ShadowForest

Author's Note

THE AUTHOR WISHES TO ACKNOWLEDGE that the notion of a shadow freezing was first suggested by Mark Twain in his book *Following the Equator.* She's also indebted to the poet William Butler Yeats, in particular for his poems "The Second Coming" and "Sailing to Byzantium."